I0718922

Felix Publishing 2020
www.felixpublishing.com.au
email: info@felixpublishing.com
Print copies available from publisher.

Letters from San Rafael

Digital Edition
ISBN: 978-1-925662-37-5
Print Edition
ISBN: 978-1-925662-36-8
Author: Dr Peter T. Scott (as Hernán Eduardo Moreno Ruiz)

Registration:
Thorpe-Bowker +61 3 8517 8342
email: bowkerlink@thorpe.com.au

This is a work of fiction. The characters in this book did not exist and the politics of the time has been generalized. Some of the places described are real and are well-known to the author. No disrespect is meant to any people living or dead in the countries of South America for which the author has a great love.

Return
to
San Rafael

Hernán Moreno Ruiz

Compiled by Dr. Peter T. Scott

To my grandchildren who are yet
to travel to the high places

Contents

Introduction

It is said that history is written by the victors and the vanquished are often forgotten. So too, are the many small events which usually fade with time, but which for a slight change in circumstances would have added them to the history books. These too are forgotten except by the men and women who participated in them. They remember!

It has been two years now since I found and published[1] the letters which Colonel Moreno had smuggled out of the fortified army supply depot of San Rafael at Baños, Ecuador. Colonel Moreno and his faithful sergeant, Garcia had been kept prisoner there following their capture during yet another border dispute between their homeland, Peru and Ecuador. Moreno had been able to smuggle letters home because many of his guards

[1] See LETTERS FROM SAN RAFAEL – Felix Publishing 2018

had relatives whose tribal lands straddled the border and were friendly to their captives. Indeed, whilst they may have been prisoners and eventually an embarrassment to the reigning junta in the capital Quito, Moreno and Garcia had been treated more like honoured guests by Comandante Castillo, the honourable old soldier who commanded at San Rafael, and his Lieutenant Gabriel Rivera.

Each of these letters contained stories told by Moreno, Garcia and the others at the hacienda of San Rafael. They told of heroes and cowards; of pride and humility; and strengths and failings of people placed in extraordinary circumstances. Finally, the last letter told the final story of the great deception which all at San Rafael had played so that Moreno, Garcia and their three wounded men could return home. The junta in Quito, who had realised that their presence was a threat to the continued uneasy relationships with Peru were none the wiser.

And so, Moreno and his men returned to Peru quietly and without the knowledge of the Ecuadorian government. It also was convenient for the high officials in Peru to forget these past events and so history was cheated of yet another interesting story.

Moreno had been quietly promoted to that of a full Coronel[2] and both he and Garcia had been placed on the inactive list of Reservists; Moreno returned to his post at the university to continue his studies whilst lecturing in Philosophy, and Garcia retired to his small farm just outside of Cuzco with the rank of Suboficial Primero.[3]

Life returned to unsettled normality for both men and their families but then history could never leave such men alone for any period of time. And so, I continued with my studies into his life in the archives of the university. He had left only a few

2 Colonel
3 Sergeant Major

records other than the letters which had been contained in a small box; mostly his academic papers and research notes. There were no more references to his military career as it had finally come to an end.

However, it was as I neared the end of my research that I discovered a small pocket notebook which had been thrown into the box of Moreno's notes. My own studies had originally been in epistemology, that branch of philosophy concerned with the study of knowledge, with specific reference to that of the Incas, but I had found Moreno's life far more interesting.

The small notebook was of the type that gentlemen would carry on their person to record the many events which occupied their daily life and which might be of some use in recording. Initially it simply was a diary of mundane events such that one would imagine from the daily life of a philosophy lecturer in a country university:

"Had lunch with Professor…noted the similarities of Parmenides to Democritus." and so on. Rather boring stuff compared to his previous letters from San Rafael which had been filled with exciting stories of the people and places he and others had visited.

In opening this small pocket notebook, a small sheet of paper fell out onto the dusty floor of the archives room. It was of a very fine texture, almost like rice paper and on it was inscribed a text written in Latin. I picked it up and immediately opened the page from which it fell and read further. Here began another series of events, people and places which reminded me of Moreno's earlier letters. I read on and so unfolded more adventures of Colonel Moreno and his friend Garcia on their return to San Rafael.

Dr. Peter T. Scott,
Cusco 2020

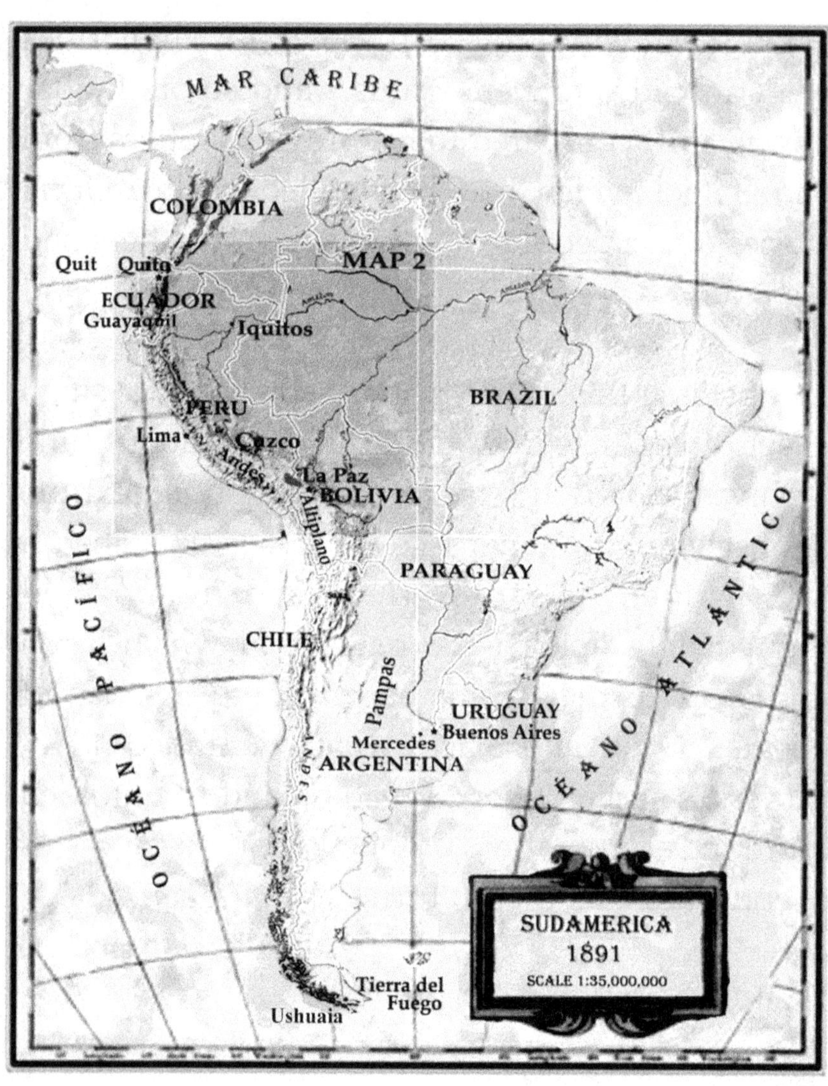

MAR CARIBE
COLOMBIA
Quit Quito
MAP 2
ECUADOR
Guayaquil
Iquitos
BRAZIL
PERU
Lima
Cuzco
La Paz
BOLIVIA
Altiplano
Andes
PARAGUAY
OCÉANO PACÍFICO
CHILE
Pampas
URUGUAY
Buenos Aires
Mercedes
ARGENTINA
OCÉANO ATLÁNTICO
SUDAMERICA
1891
SCALE 1:35,000,000
Tierra del Fuego
Ushuaia

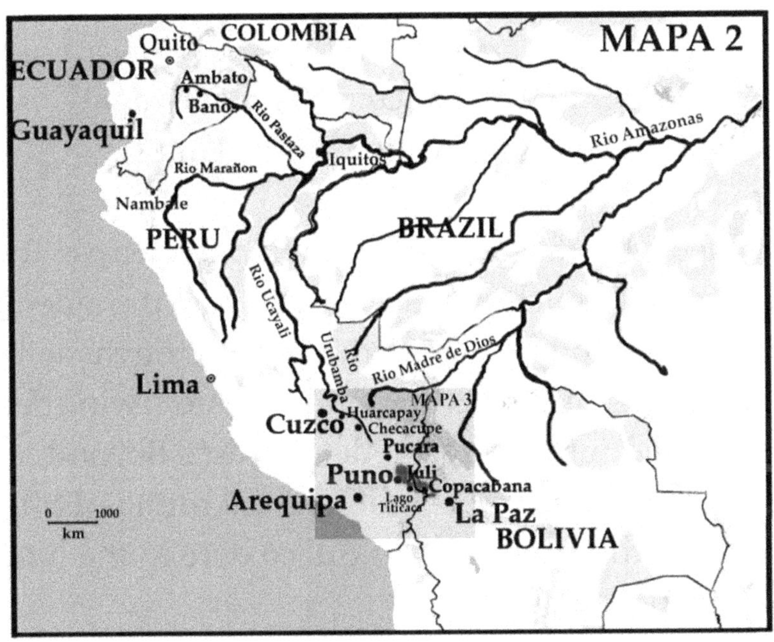

MAPA 2
COLOMBIA
ECUADOR
Quito
Ambato
Baños
Guayaquil
Rio Pastaza
Rio Marañon
Iquitos
Rio Amazonas
Nambale
PERU
BRAZIL
Rio Ucayali
Rio Urubamba
Rio Madre de Dios
Lima
MAPA 3
Cuzco
Huarcapay
Checacupe
Pucara
Puno
Juli
Copacabana
Arequipa
Lago Titicaca
La Paz
BOLIVIA
0 1000
km

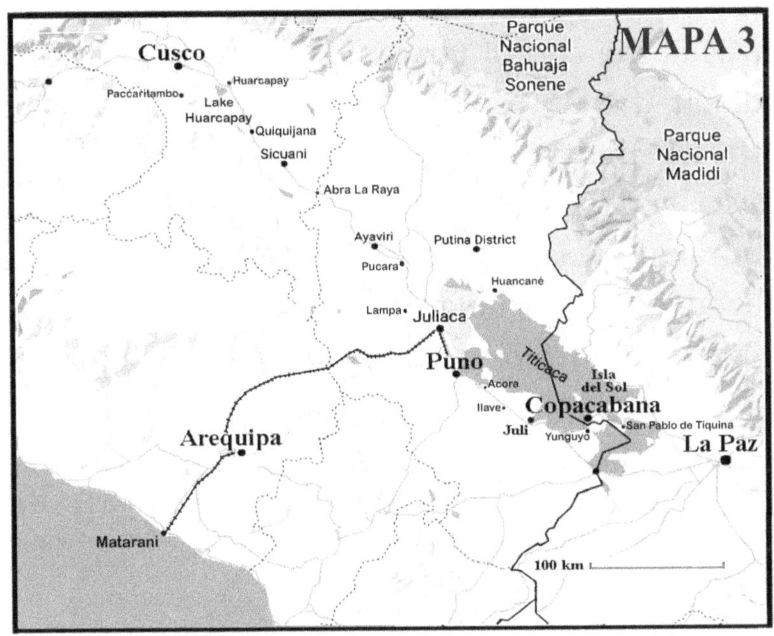

MAPA 3
Parque Nacional Bahuaja Sonene
Cusco
Huarcapay
Paccaritambo
Lake Huarcapay
Quiquijana
Parque Nacional Madidi
Sicuani
Abra La Raya
Ayaviri
Putina District
Pucara
Huancané
Lampa
Juliaca
Puno
Titicaca
Acora
Isla del Sol
Ilave
Copacabana
Juli
Yunguyo
San Pablo de Tiquina
Arequipa
La Paz
Matarani
100 km

Primera Historia: Una Vista del Lago
(First Story: A View of the Lake)

I looked out of my casement window, across the small street which wound its way past the side of the brown stone walls of the Jesuit church[1] with its Baroque architecture and ornate twin bell towers and into the Plaza de Armas[2]. Beyond, at the end of the street, I could see the rounded hills which surround the city of Cuzco here in the high mountains of Peru.

It was at the end of term, so most of the students had left the university and the small courtyard with its pretty double storey of surrounding brown and white colonnades and small central quadrangle was now empty. There would still be a few dedicated scholars who would scurry across its pebbled surface seeking the protection of the

[1] Iglesia de la Compañía de Jesús (Church of the Society of Jesus)
[2] 'Weapons Square', but better translated as Parade Square so given by the early Spanish conquerors but now used to signify the main square of many Hispanic American cities or towns.

cloisters from the biting winds which came down from those snow-covered hills.

I was in a deep mood of introspection, thinking of what I had achieved over the last few years. Certainly, my return to university life with its sheltered population of scholars and students was comforting in a way, and my domestic life also gave me much happiness. The border dispute with our neighbours to the north had again quietened down for the time being; it being a continuation of unhappiness between both countries since we had gained independence from Spain.

I also thought of my faithful companion and friend, Pablo Garcia who had been my sergeant and fellow captive in the hacienda at San Rafael. He was the professional soldier who rarely complained about his lot and usually had a greater understanding of the philosophy of humankind than I, the amateur soldier and professional philosopher. I wondered how he had settled down to domestic life as a farmer now that he had been retired from the army. We both had been of an age and in an embarrassing circumstance where it was prudent for the military to put us gently aside. Loud complaints about our captivity in Ecuador was not conducive to the fragile peace which now existed between our two countries. I had been promoted and returned to the inactive list which was enough for me. Besides, I had my own academic life to continue and there was still much to learn about the military aspects of Greek Philosophy which was my main area of study. Garcia on the other hand, would find the quiet life of farm and family very different from those many years in which he had risen in the ranks and maturity from a boy soldier fighting for his country to a Suboficial Primero.

But back to my work. I shook off the cloudiness of idle thought and went over to the small fireplace which occupied the corner of my small study. It was a cold morning and the small fire which kept out the chill from these old stone walls had started to die. I added some more coal from the copper bucket which the university in its generosity had provide and returned to my work on the writings of Xenophon, that practical-minded soldier-historian who was more sympathetic to the philosopher Socrates than many of his contemporaries.

The cold of the day was put aside as I read more of the translations of Xenophon's work until there was knock at my door.

"Enter!" I called out, as the door was of a heavy wood panelling as befitting the building which dated from the seventeenth century.

It was Sergio, the faculty's general factotum whom I had known for many years. He wore the tight jacket and undergraduate gown favoured by many of the university's non-academic staff and he held up a letter in his hand.

"Pardon, Don Hernán, but the Professor thinks that this letter may be meant for you. It is very strange."

He crossed the floor and handed me the letter, smiled with that enigmatic smile typical of Andinos[3] and gave a small bow. He was devoted to the university and regardless of the long period of our acquaintance always insisted on the formalities.

"Thank you, Sergio." I said as I turned the letter over to notice that it was addressed to 'The Soldier Philosopher'. This was quite a coincidence, considering my line of study into that other soldier – philosopher, Socrates. It was postmarked at Buenos Aires.

There are some who know me as one and others who know be as the other; few would know both aspects of my life. It the way of things that we are

[3] All people of the high Andes

often known only by one or a few facets of our individuality; only those of the most intimate of friends know of our full nature. I looked down at the letter now sitting on my desk in front of me.

"Argentina!" I thought, looking at the post mark and trying to remember whom I had known in that country. I had not been there since I was a young man. I had stayed in a small apartment on Avenida Rivadavio in the Barrio[4] Caballito and was impressed by the European buildings and broad avenues. My stay had only been brief, and whilst I had met many friendly people in that wonderful country, I was then only a young post-graduate student and was yet to join the Reserves.

Who could it be? The hand of the writer was certainly that of a scholar and someone used to writing professionally. There was not the impatient scrawl of the academic such as myself, impatient to write down thoughts which are

[4] Barrio – suburb.

travelling too fast for the hand to inscribe. Nor was it the hand of someone with a limited education where lack of practice makes the writing coarse and blocky.

I slit open the letter with the small knife which I used for such things and unfolded the crisp and rather delicate paper inside. The scholarly hand continued and I carefully read every word and every syllable trying to take in its full meaning. It read:

My Dear Friend,

It has been a long time since our last meeting and then you and our other mutual friend seemed to be a little carried away, shall we say.

Our benefactor has imparted to me privately, of some very important news which requires <u>urgent</u> attention as it is of great concern to both our countries.

It was indeed a very strange and cryptic letter. I put aside my Xenophon and took pen and paper to make some notes.

Who was our 'mutual friend?'
Why were we 'carried away?
Who was our 'benefactor?'
Where was the 'land of his birth?'
What did the reference to my mother's people and why did the 'view of the lake' concern them?
Who was 'Little Gil'?

I sat there for a considerable time trying to take in the meaning of each statement but nothing came to mind. Then it began to come together like some crazy puzzle. Such puzzles are sometimes not solved unless one stands back and take in the whole rather than the individual parts.

It came to me from the name of the sender, 'Little Gil'. Where had I heard that name before?

I remembered now. It was a story which also came from Argentina; the story of el pequeño gaucho Gill[5]. This had been told to me by Teniente[6] Gabriel Rivera Peña, the second-in-command at the Ecuadoran supply depot at San Rafael where Garcia and I had been imprisoned five years ago. Only he would know of my background and of the story of Gil the gaucho.

Now the rest of the puzzle unfolded: 'our mutual friend' was of course the stalwart Garcia; we had been 'carried away' from San Rafael pretending to be dead bodies following the great deception; and

[5] The little Gaucho or Gauchito (Argentinian cowboy), Gil.
[6] Lieutenant

our 'benefactor' could only be our good friend, the honourable soldier, Comandante Antonio Castillo Andrés who commanded at San Rafael. Of course, the 'land of his birth' was Argentina, where this letter had been posted.

There was only one obscure reference to solve; that of my 'mother's people' and their 'view of the lake '. There had been no lake anywhere near San Rafael, high in the mountains in Ecuador at Baños de Agua Santa[7].

Teniente Rivera often spoke with me whilst I was his captive and he knew of my family background as I did his. He knew that I was a mestizo[8] and that my mother, Doña Valentina Ruiz Yupanqui, could trace her ancestry back to the Capac Incans, the highest rank of the nobility of the ancient Incan peoples. But what of the reference to 'a

[7] Translated as 'Bath of the Sacred Waters, Baños is a town of great religious significance in modern Ecuador.
[8] Of mixed Spanish and Amerindian blood – common to many in South America, especially in the Andes.

view of the lake'. My mother spoke the Incan tongue of Quechua as well as Spanish and in that language, 'a view of the lake' was 'Willakuypa sayaynin'. It made no sense as I had never heard of such a place, even after such a name could be corrupted by European concepts.

It was easy to recall the day that Garcia and I had first met the young Teniente inside the walls of San Rafael. We had suffered badly under the hands of our captor, the vicious Capitán Moralez in the jungle but had been given a totally different treatment by the honourable old soldier Comandante Castillo and his young Teniente. I remember being treated with great care and taken into the inner rooms of San Rafael and a nice comforting warm fire, soft blankets and warm food. Outside, a cold wind had been blowing off the snow of Volcán Tungurahua and down the narrow valley of the Rio Pastaza. The date had been July 23rd, only two weeks away, but where was this place where we were to meet?

My mind was racing with various possibilities. Then I tried to think from the Teniente's point of view. He was going to return to Quito and continue his studies in law. No! That would have no bearing on this matter save that it reinforced my deduction of his handwriting. He came from a well-educated family from Buenos Aires who were proud of their Spanish heritage. I therefore reasoned that his knowledge of native languages would be rather scanty to say the least. Perhaps he had mistaken my mother's native Quechua for that of another. Another common language of ancient Peru was that of the Aymara people who lived well to the south of Cuzco around Lake Titicaca. Of course! – the lake of which one would have a good view!

I raced out of my room and out onto the cloisters which surrounded the central courtyard. Down the flight of steps and across the cold, dry pebbles to the opposite side where my good friend and colleague Pedro Pérez Navia had his study. He came from Puno in that region and I knew that both of his parents were of the Aymara people. But was he in his rooms?

Without knocking I burst into his study to find my friend sitting at his desk, now startled at this sudden intrusion.

"Pedro! Quick! What is the Aymara for the phrase 'a view of the lake'?"

Now composed he gave me that enigmatic smile and look that one would give to a small child asking a stupid question.

'Why, Hernán, that is very well-known to my people. It is kota kahuana, the name the misinformed give to the town of Copacabana in Bolivia. However, some say that the name of the town was actually named after Kotakawana, the goddess of fertility in ancient Andean mythology, the equivalent to the classical Greek goddess Aphrodite. But this may have been unacceptable to the early God-fearing Spanish," he laughed.

So! I now knew the location where Gabriel Rivera desired us to meet and the date. However, there was one last piece of the puzzle which I could not understand; that was the reference to 'Viva Nueva España!'[9]

At the time of our last meeting, I did not think that the young Teniente was overly patriotic; and then not to the country which his countrymen had fought so hard to expel in the fight for independence. He was a young officer in the army of Ecuador but had been born and raised in Argentina, so why this reference to our former occupiers? It had been a deliberate but cryptic statement, but what did it mean?

I returned to Pedro's study but this time at a less feverish pace. Perhaps he might find some connection between the Teniente's statement and the town of Copacabana. I knocked on his door and entered.

[9] 'Long Live Spain!'

"Ah! The return of the cryptic Don Hernán!" he exclaimed.

"Pedro" I asked, "is there any connection between the expression 'Viva Nueva España!' and Copacabana?

Pedro looked puzzled for a moment and bade me to sit whilst he went to his bookcase and extracted a small volume.

"Perhaps it was not a reference to your correspondent's patriotism but perhaps a time or a place. Bolivia gained its independence from Spain on August 6, 1825. Does that date make any sense?"

"No." I replied, "he gave me a cryptic date which was very definite in its translation, so I doubt that it would be a time nor date. Your view that it might be a place has some merit, but he very specifically referred to Copacabana. Would there be a place in that town to which the statement might ring true?"

Pedro consulted his slim volume which I noted was a modern almanac on Bolivia. He thumbed through a few pages muttering to himself in that manner which many academics have when they are thinking about a serious problem.

"Ah!" he suddenly cried, "here it is, I am certain of it! The 'Posada[10] Nueva España' is a small family hotel in Copacabana on Calle[11] Michel Pérez. I know the area well. I was there many years ago, but I know that the street is on the hill which leads up to the Cerro El Calvario[12]. This is where your friend might be staying."

So now the puzzles of the Teniente's letter were complete. I would meet him at the Posada Nueva España in Copacabana, Bolivia on July 23rd.

---

[10] Posada – an inn, usually run by a family.
[11] Street
[12] The Hill of the Calvary – a religious shrine to the east of the city.

Segunda Historia: Otra Expedición
(Second Story: Another Exploration)

Teniente Rivera's letter seemed important enough for him to contact me and also because it was coded in such a way that only I would understand its meaning and that others may be watching. As it was the end of Term, I resolved, then to go to Copacabana and find the meaning of his urgency.

Copacabana was well to the south of Cuzco, on the southern edges of Lake Titicaca. It was not far from the southern Peruvian town of Puno where I had once visited during my brief military career at the end of the War of the Pacific when Chilean forces had occupied Peruvian territory. It brought back old memories of almost fifteen years ago.

When the city of Puno had been threatened by the Chileans and the remnants of his army had fled north into the rugged hills beyond Lake Titicaca, I had been put on active duty and given command of a company of men to march south and assist in the reorganisation of Peru's defences. I was only a Mayor[1] in the Reserves then, and had no doubts that this was a fruitless adventure. Never-the-less I had gathered a mixture of administrative staff, new conscripts and patriotic volunteers and marched south. Our three-hundred-kilometre route was along the old road through the high valleys which connected Cuzco, the capital of the old Incan Empire to its traditional heartland on the lake. This had also been a personal journey for me as it was the country of my mother's people who could trace her ancestry back to the Capac Incans. It was also on this expedition that I had met Sargento Pablo Garcia Lorca.

The Sargento and I had met near the little village of Pucara just north of the Lake. Garcia had collected the remnants of his men after most of his officers had been killed or captured and had welcomed the arrival of my rag-tag company. He

---

[1] Major – the terms 'mayor' and 'major' are used interchangeably in this book depending upon how it is spoken.

had a better understanding of how to fight using the land rather than in set piece engagements and he had also gathered some of the local people who had formed themselves into small, militia bands which were useful in harassing the formal patrols of the enemy now that Puno had been occupied. There had been little contact with Chilean forces and our small outpost had little to do but patrol the northern part of the Lake and live as best we could. Garcia and I had come to appreciate each other despite our differences in social class and rank. I admired Garcia as the professional soldier who led his Andino soldiers with a strong but friendly pragmatism and I felt that he, in turn saw that I was an officer who was also prepared to learn the arts of war and truly cared for our men. There was also a common bond between us; the mountain upbringing of the soldier and his officer. Garcia was surprised that I, with a classical education and with a wider knowledge of the world than anyone that he had known, could speak fluent Quechua[2] and knew the customs of the people of the mountains. I remember his surprise when he offered me a hot cup of mate de coca[3] on a cold winter's night and I poured a little onto the ground as the traditional offering to Pachamama, the Incan Earth mother.

Whatever the urgency of this matter, and the Teniente's reference to our 'mutual friend' who could only be Garcia, I felt that such a new adventure also warranted the talents of my old companion.

Garcia and his wife, Constanza and their two children now lived on a small farm just outside of Cuzco. After he had retired from the army, he had moved his family down from his village in the north and had settled in Cuzco hoping to find work. Times had been tough in the city after the

[2] Pronounced "ketch-uwah" is the language of the Incas and many other peoples of the Andes. Called the Runa Simi in their language.
[3] An excellent traditional herbal tea still used today and made from the coca bush. It is very useful for altitude sickness.

war and but he had bought a small farm near the village of Yuncaypata, in the hills just north of the city.

I had discussed the letter and its probable meaning with Louisa, my wife and asked for her opinion. We had often shared these conversations when I was an Exploring Officer during the many border disputes and she knew the risks which I had taken. My imprisonment in San Rafael had been a very troublesome time for her and I now gave her reassurance that this new venture would be only a slight diversion from our settled life. Little did I know.

The next day, I rode up into the hills and past the ruins of Inkilltambo and along the edge of the small plateau which led up to the village of Yuncaypata. Garcia's small farm was built on the edge of the plateau – a soldier's position – with a fine view to the north and several cultivated terraces which would get the northern sun. The farm buildings were typical of the region; a high mud-brick walled rectangular enclosure with its buildings inside. The main structure was a large, two-story building made of the same dried mud bricks in the far corner of the enclosure. There was another, single storey building in the adjacent corner. The courtyard was accessed through a large double gate which had sturdy wooden doors which could be closed at night.

As I approached the farm, Garcia's two dogs came running and barking down the path. It was near noon by the time I had arrived and luckily, I had found Garcia and his family at home. Garcia was the first to come out of the home compound typical of such farms. It surrounded the main two-storey adobe house with its red tiled roof and the several out buildings which hugged the inside walls of the compound.

He carried his hoe, suspicious of any stranger approaching his home but when he saw me riding up his road, he dropped it suddenly and ran up to my side; his dogs barking excitedly beside him.

"Mi Coronel, Mi Coronel" he cried, "is it you?"

"Who else would climb all of this way up to this farm to see my old friend? Garcia. You are looking well!" I replied.

I climbed down off my horse and we embraced in the old style of the mountains. He had tears in his eyes as he wished me welcome and beckoned me up to his house.

"Come! Come! Patrón[4], Constanza and the boys will be glad to see you again." He laughed.

We walked together up to the house where Constanza and her three sons were standing on the balcony of the upper floor. Once they recognised who the mystery horseman was, the boys ran down the stairs and out into the yard. They gathered around Garcia and me as we came through the gate.

[4] Patron or more colloquially "Boss" – a mark of respect.

"Don Hernán! Don Hernán! Antonio the eldest cried. He was a sturdy boy of about sixteen and stocky like his father. His two younger brothers, Juan who was fourteen and his ten-year-old brother, Rodrigo were also pleased to see me. Constanza stood at the foot of the stairs with the half smile which many army wives had when greeting their husband's former officer for such a meeting in the past had meant that her husband was called yet again for another military exploration.

I greeted her with a low bow and took her hand. There were never any falsehoods between Garcia's wife and I; she always knew when I would require her husband, my trusty Sargento Primero for yet another mission to gather intelligence for the army.

"So! you had better come into the house, Don Hernán and tell us of your latest tale," she said with a wry smile. "We had thought that you had given up your adventures."

Garcia and I walked arm-in-arm to the stairs and then followed his wife up to the main room of their house. I ducked my head under the low door as I was taller than most of the local people, having had a father with Spanish blood.

It was a large room and comfortable. It had a large family table and chairs constructed simply out of local wood and there was a small santuario[5] in one corner of the room with a statue of the Virgin and some flowers. Garcia opened the door of a side cupboard and produced a bottle of wine and two glasses. Constanza left the room with a comment about 'men's business' and her boys laughed and followed her down the stairs. Garcia looked apprehensive across the table.

"Indeed, it is 'men's business' which I have come to talk to you about Garcia, but as yet, I too, know little about what it may mean." I told him about the letter from our former gaoler and friend

5 Small religious shrine

Teniente Rivera Peña and how he had subtly suggested that Garcia and I should meet with him in Copacabana in Bolivia.

Garcia was excited. The life of the farmer had been too quiet of late for someone who had spent most of his life as a professional soldier. Of course, he made all of the excuses about the needs of his family but I could tell that he would be willing to go. I expressed my own doubts about where our new adventure would take us and the unknown length of our adventure. So far it seemed like a simple meeting with our old friend in a neighbouring country with people of similar kinship and good intensions. It was only the cryptic nature of Gabriel Rivera's letter which gave me some concern.

At the end of our short conversation and a few glasses of his excellent chicha[6], Garcia took another quick glass, raised his finger to the side of

[6] A corn beer usually brewed at home.

his nose and went to the door. Half turning and looking at me with uncertainty, he opened his mouth as if to give a reason for his departure but thought better of it and quickly left. I could only image what excuses he would give to his wife, but I was certain that Constanza would scold him briefly and then resign herself to yet another departure of the man she knew always came back.

It was some time before he again appeared in the doorway. I had almost felt that this time his wife would prevail; after all, Garcia was no longer a soldier although like myself he was still on the Reserve list and drew his pension.

He came into the room with that satisfied grin which he usually had when things were going well for him.

"We go, mi Coronel! You and I again!" he said with considerable animation, throwing a small pack onto the table which contained the few belongings which he would need on our trip. As a soldier, he had always travelled with few belongings; a change of clothing, a water-proof poncho, a water skin and a little food would be the only supplement he would need for his well-worn Sergeant's uniform. Now he was dressed in more sober clothing of brown hand-woven trousers and shirt and his beloved poncho. He also carried a wide-brimmed hat and only his sturdy military boots distracted from the dress of a local farmer from the Cuzco region. He looked up and gave me a depreciating grin.

"She understands, "he said with an uplift of both hands as if to offer an explanation which would not come in words. He had had this conversation with his wife on many occasions.

"Besides," he continued, "she now has three strong sons to help her with the farm for the short time that I will be gone."

This last comment was one of optimism for Garcia always knew that our time away from our families on our military explorations were always uncertain. Our last mission had only been to our country's northern border, yet we had spent many months as prisoners in the hacienda San Rafael and we had only returned because of the friendship and cunning of our gaolers who had become our friends. Now it was to honour that friendship that we were to answer the call of one of them; Teniente Gabriel Rivera Peña.

Tercera Historia: El Cuento de García
(Third Story: Garcia's Tale)

I stayed the night at Garcia's farm; I slept in the upstairs bedroom normally occupied by his three sons whilst they were made comfortable in the small barn below which was normally occupied by their cow, Esmeralda. My bed was much too small for a good night's rest and the expectations and doubts about our journey also did not help.

Garcia, as was his custom, had gone into the village to buy soft bread rolls to have with our coffee for our breakfast. The boys were also up and dashing around the house, excited to have a guest under their roof.

Garcia and I were silent at breakfast with Constanza bringing our food and coffee. There was little to be said except a sad farewell to his wife and sons and we left as soon as breakfast was over. Antonio had saddled my horse and his father's mule Juanita, and with a final wave of his hand, Garcia yet again left his family for a new adventure.

The track down to the valley of Cuzco was steep at first as we slowly made our way down the valley along the road near the small creek which ran past the ancient terraces and ruins of Inkilltambo. It was here on the slopes of the hills which led down to the city that the Inca's people had planted their crops in multiple terraces; engineered gardens which carried water down from the hills and which faced to the northwest to get every benefit from Inti, their god of the Sun.

It was probably not more than about ten kilometres from my home on the Avenida el Sol, not far from my university and the Plaza de Armas, but it took us most of the morning to make the trip. It was, of course a very leisurely ride as Garcia and I had much to talk about since our last meeting and especially about our stay at the hacienda San Rafael those many years ago.

Eventually we passed through the gates of my home and into the main courtyard. Joaquim my stable hand took our mounts to be unsaddled, brushed down and stabled whilst Garcia and I walked through to the inner courtyard with its fruit trees and fountain. We were met here by Ambrosio, my man-servant and general factotum[1].

"Welcome home, Don Hernán, and you too, Sargento Garcia!" He said with a broad smile. Ambrosio had been my batman when I occasionally lived within the army barracks and he and Garcia were old friends. He was a man of many talents I had found. The happy and smiling friend as he was now, to the sombre and formal man-servant when formality demanded a neutral appearance. He could almost make himself invisible in a crowd of dignitaries and officers yet he knew and heard everything. There were few secrets that Ambrosio could not discern.

[1]Household servant who did all manner of things.

My wife Christina came down the stairs from our apartments and greeted us both warmly; a caress and a kiss for me and an acceptance of Garcia's hand.

"Good day, Doña Christina." Garcia said with a low bow, for he had been a family friend since we had first met during the war.

"You are most welcome, Don Pablo," She replied with her usual enigmatic smile. Garcia blushed slightly at this courteous use of his Christian name. Christina valued my friendship with Garcia for she knew that there was no other man able to best protect her husband than this honest and experienced soldier. "Come, for there is food on our table and we would like to hear about Constanza and your family. I must apologise however, as our eldest son Mateo is away at the Military Academy. But Andrés and Alejandra have been looking forward to your stories. You are staying tonight?" she asked, turning to me with pleading eyes.

"Yes, my love. Garcia and I will stay overnight and take the morning coach south tomorrow morning. I am sure that he can scare the children with some of his stories tonight, yes Garcia?"

We enjoyed a sumptuous lunch of chicken soup, rocoto relleno[2], a fine solterito[3] and a dessert of a crema volteada[4] washed down with a fine wine.

After this excellent lunch, as was our custom, we spent the rest of the afternoon in relaxation: Garcia and I in the inner courtyard under the trees with a fine cigar and my wife and the children in their rooms.

Later that afternoon, Garcia and I strolled up the Avenida el Sol to the Plaza de Armas. We walked

[2] Peppers stuffed with beef, olives, onions, herbs and topped with grilled cheese.
[3] Chopped salad of lima beans, fresh cheese, chili pepper, tomatoes and large kernel native corn.
[4] "Upside-down creme," is based on the classic French recipe for crème caramel often with quinoa, raisins and nuts.

past the Iglesia de la Compañía de Jesús[5] and into the grounds of the university and to my rooms across the courtyard. Here I gathered a few papers which may be useful to us on our journey, mainly a letter of introduction to the Professor of Classics at the University of the Altiplano[6] in Puno; a good cover story for our need to travel to this city.

That evening, after a light dinner consisting of an array of bread with ham, cheese, roasted corn and eggs with glasses of juice and chicha, Christina and I retired to our main room whilst Garcia took Andrés and Alejandra to my study to tell them a story. My study had a nice fire burning in the grate and Ambrosio had lit only a few candles for he knew that Garcia always liked the appropriate setting for one of his famous stories.

[5] Jesuit Church

[6] Altiplano – the 'High Plains" of the Andes or really a series of parallel valleys over three thousand metres above sea level.

With the children seated in front of the fire, Garcia sat upon a small footstool and told them the story of how the Inca was born. All of my children had heard this story before from their mother, who like mine could trace her ancestry back to that culture which had made Cuzco their capital. Garcia would probably know this, but it was one of his favourite stories and he had the gift of drama which could make even the most peaceful fairy-tale into one of death, destruction and horror. The kind of tales which children like to hear at night. His story went like this:

"Once there was only darkness in this world and it was very cold with no fire like we have in this nice warm room" Garcia began his story and the two children snuggled up closer to each other and looked around them in the semi-darkness of the study.

"There was a great flood which also covered the land," he continued "some say it came from Lake Titicaca which is to our south. Others say that the lake is only what has been left when the flood was dried up by Inti the Sun.

After Inti had dried up this flood, four brothers and their wives came out of a dark cave called Paqariq Tampu[7] where they had been hiding. This cave was on a hill called Tampu T'uqu or the 'cave of three windows'. The entrances were called Maras T'uqu, Qhapaq T'uqu and Sutiq T'uqu".

The children mouthed each new word for they were difficult to pronounce and their mother had only just begun to teach them how to speak in Runasimi, the Quechua tongue.

Garcia, who had learnt this story from his mother many years ago and knew every detail in the language of his birth continued:

[7] From the Quechua for "dwelling place of the dawn" or "place of birth"

"You know, children, there is a town which the Spaniards called Paccarictambo which is not far to our south. Perhaps this is where these people came from?"

"But Tio[8] Pablo!" Andrés questioned as he always wanted to know the truth about everything he had heard. "Did they not come from the sacred island in Lake Titicaca?"

"Indeed." Garcia replied, "some say that they came from a cave on the Isla del Sol[9], where Inti the Sun was born. This was after his father Viracocha Pachayachachi, the Creator of All Things had made him and his two sisters Mama Killa, the Moon and Pachamama, the Earth mother and brought light to the world.

But then Viracocha was not satisfied with the common people he had created so he sent a great

8 Tio – Spanish for 'Uncle'
9 Island of the Sun

flood around the lake and saved only the people who emerged from the caves.

"What were these people called, Tio Pablo?" asked Alejandra who was the youngest.

"They were called the brothers Ayar" replied Garcia "and their names were Ayar Manco, Ayar Kachi and Ayar Uchu. Their wives were called Mama Uqllu, Mama Cora, and Mama Rahua.

Now Manco was the eldest brother and he had many names. Some later called him 'Manco Inka' which meant 'the ruler' but he was also known as Manqu Qhapaq[10] which means the 'royal founder' because he is thought to be the founder of the Incan people whose city was Cuzco. Some say that he was also the son of Inti the Sun.

Manco, his three brothers and their wives came out of the cave of the three windows through the

[10] Also written as Manco Cápac in Spanish and considered by some to be a real leader of the Incas in the thirteenth century.

main middle window which was called qhapaq t'uqu. Now the brother Ayar Kachi possessed enormous strength, and would throw huge stones right up to the sky using his sling. The stones fell back to the ground and caused great damage. He was also very cruel to the common people who Viracocha had also created and had come out of the side caves and this made the other brothers and their wives very sad. He was a bully, but like many of this kind of person, he was also not very bright, so the other brothers decided to trick him. They called him and asked to go back into the cave to fetch some important items which they would need: the golden vases called tupac-cusi, some sacred seeds, and above all the napa, a sacred white llama with a red body cloth, on the top, ear-rings of gold and a breast plate with red badges.

At first Ayar Kachi would not go back; he was also a lazy young man who cared little for others. But Mama Uqllu scolded him for being a coward and not wanting to do as his brothers asked. So, he returned to the caves of Tampu T'uqu along with a companion who the other brothers had chosen and had ordered to kill Ayar Kachi. When they reached the caves, Ayar Kachi entered to fetch the sacred objects and the companion sealed the cave with a huge rock. It was even said that the loud curses of Ayar Kachi within turned this companion to a rock also.

So, the three brothers and the four wives travelled towards the place where Cuzco now stands, planting crops and helping the people along the way. Ayar Uchu wanted to stay back to watch over the people, and it was after promising to help them in the future that he was instantly turned to stone to be a sacred place called a huaca where the people could come and make their requests.

Ayar Manco continued on with the three wives and all of the people he had gathered to follow him. Finally, he came to the lovely valley of Cuzco where he planted his golden staff and declared that this would be his people's new home. But first they had to overcome the people who already lived in the valley. In the battle that ensued between the people who lived there, and Ayar Manco's force, he came out victorious, and eventually founded the Incan Empire. This was when he was called Manqu Qhapaq - the 'royal founder'. And remember that both your mother and your father can trace their people back to the Incan nobility.

Well, did you like that story?" Garcia asked the children.

"We've heard it before, Tio Pablo," said Andrés, "but you tell it much better than Mama".

"Oh yes!" said little Alejandra," I like the part where Ayer Kachi was sealed up in the cave. All bullies should be treated that way!" she said, taking a stern sideways glance at Andrés. "Can we have another story please, Tio Pablo?"

Garcia stood up from the little foot stool and stretched his arms up over his head and yawn.

"I am afraid it is time that we all went to bed. Your father and I must go on our journey tomorrow and you must go to school. So, I will say 'good night' to both of you." With that he ushered the sleepy children out of the room and to where their mother was waiting on the balcony.

Cuarta Historia: El Guerrero y El Sacerdote
(Fourth Story: The Warrior and the Priest)

The next morning, Maria our cook, brought breakfast early; simple soft pastry and coffee with an egg for Garcia. It was a silent affair as the parting from my family weighed heavily on my shoulders and even the natural excitement of my friend could not raise my spirits. After breakfast we retired to our rooms to make ready for our journey.

Entering my room, I found Ambrosio laying out my travelling clothes.

"I took the liberty, Don Hernán, of laying out your leather waistcoat and your expedition necessities." He said looking over his glasses with serious eyes. Very little escaped Ambrosio in this house and he had the soldier's intuition when there was something amiss. The waistcoat to which he referred was indeed made of good, soft leather but it had a decorative linen front piece which made it appear as a normal waistcoat when worn below my normal long coat. It varied from any other gentleman's waistcoat however, in having a pistol holster under the left arm and a long pouch for ammunition under the right. There was also a small throwing knife inserted into my boot. I had worn this armoury on several occasions when my missions as an Exploration Officer with the army required me to travel, in part at least, as a civilian; normally it would have been protocol to explore in full uniform.

"Thank you, Ambrosio" I smiled, "as usual you have anticipated my needs and thought of everything."

I noted that he had also fitted my Smith & Wesson Hammerless 0.38 model with the longer barrel. This was a pocket pistol which would not make such a bulge under my coat and the longer barrel would give me more accuracy. I had several pistols in my arsenal which I kept securely locked in a hidden compartment in the bookcase in my study. On my usual explorations, I carried a .45 Schofield revolver in my side holster instead of the usual handgun issued by the army. I also had a long-barrel Remington repeating rifle in my saddle holster. My cavalry sabre and an ugly Bowie knife in a scabbard at the back of my belt completed my 'field equipment'. These too were locked away in my study armoury along with considerable ammunition as I had found that extracting specialised ammunition from Army Ordinance was a nightmare of paperwork. No, Ambrosio was correct in his selection of traveling weapons.

Garcia, on the other hand looked relatively peaceful in his manservant's uniform which Ambrosio had also provided and somewhat scholarly in the pair of plain-glass round spectacles which he had insisted that Garcia should wear as part of his disguise. There had been some argument about this between the two old friends, but Garcia finally saw the need for him to keep in the background as my servant and scribe. As such, he would be seen as carrying no weapons, but I knew however that he carried a longer version of my Bowie knife in a padded sling under his left armpit a smaller knife concealed in his right boot top and two throwing knifes in a broad holder on the upper back just below the nape of the neck which was therefore very accessible. He also had prodigious strength and I pity any man who would tangle with Garcia in some darkened alleyway!

It was still early when Joaquim loaded our two light travelling bags and a small valise of papers onto our trap. After a farewell from my wife and my two children, we headed off down the Avenida El Sol to the Coaching Station of the Posada de Los Angeles at Wanchaq. It would be here that we would catch the early morning coach which headed south to Puno which was over three hundred kilometres and perhaps four to five days. At least our road was good as there was British company building the new railway line between the two cities and the road had been repaired. Moreover, it was a direct route along the Altiplano between the mountain ranges and there would only be the easy pass at La Raya which could give the horses some difficulty.

Ambrosio had managed to secure two seats on the morning coach to Puno. It was a simple 'four-in-hand'[1] coach, what the North American's would call a 'stagecoach' which would stop at designated coaching inns along the way. Joaquim handed our two travelling bags to the driver who was carefully loading the top and rear seats of the coach for it appeared that we had a full load. The ostlers had harnessed the four horses at the front of the coach ensuring that we would soon be on our way.

There were only four of us travelling south this morning; an older army officer in the uniform of an Infantry Major; a priest of indeterminable age, Garcia and I.

[1] A four-in-hand is a carriage drawn by a hitch of four horses having the lines rigged in such a way that it can be driven by a single driver.

As Garcia walked around to supervise the loading of our bags onto the top of the coach, I was approached by the army officer.

"Señor," he said in a quiet, conspiratorial voice, "your manservant - he is not travelling on top?"

I turned to him and was able to hide the flash of anger in my eyes. This was the first test of our need to travel incognito and so I assumed my guise as the harmless travelling academic.

"Señor?" I replied.

"Your manservant," the officer repeated," he is an Indian and perhaps should ride up top at the rear of the coach."

I innocently looked up at the rear of the coach, shading my eyes from the morning sun. The rear seats were already packed with two large campaign trunks, the type used by army officers in their travels. Turning back to the Major, I meekly replied: "My pardon señor, normally that would be the case, but he is also my clerk as well as my servant. For an Indian he is well educated, and there may be a need for him to help me with my papers en route. I hope that this will not be an inconvenience to you?"

The officer gave a dissatisfied snort and turned away quickly to climb into the carriage. The priest followed him, I then climbed in so that Garcia would not have the inconvenience of sitting opposite this upstart officer.

Having been settled in the coach, the ostler closed the door before we started our long journey south.

Garcia, true to form as an experienced soldier played his role as a meek and studious manservant and kept his eyes low and gazed out at the passing scene as the couch trundled its way down the dusty highway which wound through the narrow hills which formed a natural funnel at the end of the valley which contained our city. Soon this would open up into one of the narrow valleys or series of parallel flats which formed the Altiplano. We would soon be under the shelter of rocky, snow-covered mountains on either side. Regardless of the fact that we were almost at four thousand metres above sea level, these majestic peaks seemed to reach almost to the sky.

"Sed et si ambulavero in valle altissimis tenebris premuntur, non timebo mala, quoniam tu mecum[2]." Said the priest quietly as he closed the Bible which he had opened after gaining his seat.

"A beautiful piece from the Twenty-third Psalm, Padre." I replied looking into his strong face.

"You know your Latin and your scriptures, my son." he replied with a smile.

---

[2] "Even though I walk through the darkest valley, I will fear no evil, for you are with me" (Psalm 23:4 part)

"A waste of time, Latin!" said the fastidious Major who was now brushing the first thin coating of dust from the blue serge of his uniform jacket. "A dead language only useful for priests with nothing to say and doctors who say too much."

"You have no Latin?" the priest asked.

"No!" he replied sharply "I am a soldier and deal in plain speech and words of command. I have no need for the mutterings of ancient languages. And you, señor?" he said turning to me, "you seem to understand the Padre's doggerel!"

"Yes, Mayor, I understand some Latin, but I would hardly consider it one of my talents," I replied with the meekest tone which I could muster.

"And pray tell, what are your talents, señor?" he asked belligerently.

"I am a philosopher from the university and I sometimes have to read Latin to find out what some of the ancient scholars wished to impart to us poor souls of this modern world."

Garcia moved slightly, showing his discomfort but continued to look out of the window at the small farms and the people in the fields who were more of his world than that of the rest of us.

"I have little time for scholars and their safe little worlds. I am a soldier and deal with the practical tactics of warfare which keep your little worlds safe."

The priest put his Bible into the pocket of his cassock and folded his arms, eyes downwards but his mind no doubt on our conversation.

"You have seen many battles, then Mayor?" I asked, regretting now that I had risen slightly to his arrogance.

"Many! I was on the staff of Don Nicolás de Piérola at the defense of our beloved capital during the War of the Pacific[3]" he replied smugly dusting a small insect off the gold braid of one of his cuffs.

"Well, now! That is indeed wonderful!" I said in my best tone of appreciation for I knew from my own military experience that this blusterer would have been one of the many senior officers who fled to the mountains with our former President leaving the remnants of our depleted army at the barricades after losing over thirty percent of our men. "And where now are you headed, Mayor? There is now peace between Peru and Chile."

"My mission is of course highly secret, but I must travel to our military headquarters at Huarcapay to inspect the garrison and judge the situation there. So, I am sorry that I shall be leaving you

[3] Fought between Chile and a Peruvian-Bolivian alliance from 1879 to 1884 after Chile had invaded western Bolivia and annexed its coastal region, rich in minerals.

within a few hours. Otherwise I could tell you of a few campaigns which I am sure you would indeed find wonderful." This was said with a smile of deep self-satisfaction.

For my part and for the tolerance of my companions, I was grateful that our foolish Major would soon be leaving, for Huarcapay was only about fifteen kilometres south of Cuzco in a relatively quiet region noted for its lake and wildlife. It was also just a short distance from where the Urubamba River emerges from its mountainous course and flows down into the valley that would be our route. From the Major's nature, age, immaculate uniform and his collar insignia of the General Staff, I could deduce that his 'battles' were mainly fought using ledgers and other 'weapons' of administration and that his 'secret mission' would probably be a random audit of the small, local garrison at Huarcapay. I pity their Commanding Officer who would no doubt suffer under the tongue of this pompous individual.

Unfortunately, like many of his ilk, the fastidious major put his head back on the hard rest at the top of the even harder seat with his kepi[4] half over his eyes and continued with his stories of his 'campaigns'. Most of them were exaggerations of some of the events of the War of the Pacific which our brave warrior would have heard in the Officers' Mess in the safe walls of Headquarters in Lima.

The padre had again taken out his Bible and put his head down in the guise of reading, but I had noted that he had opened the book at random. Garcia had given the fastidious major a venomous look but again turned to look out of the coach window and tried to shut his professional soldier's mind from the nonsense which came from our story-teller. I had also shut off my mind to his nonsense but occasionally gave him a benign smile. Perhaps silence would have been a better tactic. The coach rattled on down the

[4] A military cap with a flat circular top and a peak.

highway and the dust settled even deeper on its occupants.

Eventually after what seemed more like a full day than a few scant hours, our coach arrived at the posada which acted as the staging inn at the village of Huarcapay. A small trap[5] pulled by an old mule, was waiting in front of the posada. On the driver's seat was a soldier wearing the dusty uniform of an Infantry Cabo[6] and whose head was bowed in slumber. He suddenly came to life as we pulled in. He made a quick attempt at brushing the dust of his red pantaloons and jumped down from the trap and gave the semblance of a salute as the priest and then the major alighted from the coach.

The fastidious major made a show of patting the dust off his uniform then went over to the Cabo and returned the salute with some degree of smartness. After a terse conversation at which the

[5] a light, two-wheeled carriage.
[6] Lance Corporal

Cabo stood more erect and straightened his drab uniform, came another salute; much smarter this time. The major climbed up onto the trap without any social farewells nor any sign of wishing to take refreshment at the posada. The Cabo hurried to unload the major's two trunks from the upper rear seat with the help of an ostler who had suddenly emerged from the courtyard. Garcia and I followed the old priest into the posada and found a cool bench under one of the trees in the inner courtyard. The priest came over, walking with a steady, upright tread but with a slight limp with some small assistance of a long, thin walking cane. He sat down at the end of the bench and smiled.

"Perhaps it is time for some introductions" he said with a smile and he extended his hand. The grip was unexpectedly firm. "I am Father Xavier, and I am happy to meet you now that our heroic friend has departed," he continued with a slight chuckle.

"The pleasure is mine for both circumstances." I replied. "Allow me to introduce myself as Doctor Hernán Vázquez." I lied, giving my grandfather's family name, "and this is my manservant and scribe as well as my friend Pablo."

Garcia smiled, taking off his broad hat and giving an uncertain bow "Good day, Padre."

Father Xavier gave a conspiratorial smile and said "I did not think for a moment that your friend was a mere servant or you an academic. I have had too many dealings with a great variety of people in my profession señor, not to recognise a military man when I see one," he laughed at the look of surprise on my face. Garcia looked at me with some uncertainty. A servant of the posada brought us a jug of cool lemon water and some glasses then hurried off.

"You are most observant, Padre. Both Pablo and I have served in the military but that now is behind us. However, I really am a lecturer in Philosophy at the university in Cuzco, so you have missed that point." I smiled. "But allow me to make my own observations also, Padre. I see by the quality and style of your cassock or should I call it your Soutane[7] that you are a member of the Society of Jesus[8]? I suspect also, that like the founder of your Order that you too have had some military training, yes?"

The old priest laughed. "What is it that the French say? - 'touché!' Don Hernán. Yes, you are right. In my youth I was a soldier but I found God's calling more to my liking than the trumpet call of battle. But I see that they have finished changing the horses and that it is time to go. Shall we?"

He stood up, erect as ever and with a slight bow turned and walked back to our coach.

---

[7] Soutane – the style of cassock similar to a robe which is wrapped around the body and was tied with a cincture or rope-like belt, rather than the customary buttoned front. Their hat or Biretta also does not have its surmounted tuft.

[8] A Jesuit – a Roman Catholic order founded in 1540 by Ignatius of Loyola, a former soldier.

Quinta Historia: Montañas y Sirenas
(Fifth Story: Mountains and Mermaids)

No one else had taken passage from Huarcapay, so now there were only the three of us in the coach as it resumed its dusty journey down the highway south to Puno.

A short distance down the road, we passed an immense area of wetlands and lagoons consisting of a large lake edged by totora reeds[1]; a flock of white Ibis took flight from its foreshore.

Father Xavier leaned across and said "That is Lake Huarcapay, Don Hernán. It is noted for its wildlife but there is a darker side to its beauty." He continued as I looked up at him surprise. "Some of the locals claim that the lake is a place of dread. The say that people who have ventured out onto the water have often not returned and

---

[1] Totora reeds - *Schoenoplectus californicus* subsp. *tatora* is a subspecies of the giant bulrush found in South America, notably on Lake Titicaca and other parts.

that the lake is inhabited by Umantuus and other monsters who come out at night."

"Umantuus?" I enquired.

"Yes. What our European ancestors would call 'mermaids'. They have the usual body of a man or woman but the hind section of a fish. However, our local mermaids are of the freshwater variety and inhabit only lakes and streams; they are not the Pincoy who are their cousins who live in the seas. They are sometimes called 'sirena' as in the sirens of ancient Greece and in the province of Lampa, not far from Puno, close to Lake Titicaca, there are several places named Sirenayoc which combines this Spanish word 'sirena' and the Quechua word 'yoc' for 'who owns', so the total meaning is 'where there are mermaids'. In Chile, they are also called 'Coñi Lafquen' or Lake Maidens and are said to have long, golden hair which they brush in the moonlight and are said to lure unsuspecting young fishermen from their reed boats. They are said to also inhabit Lake

Titicaca and are the servants of the god who lives under the water."

"Kotakawana" I replied.

"Ah! I see you know something of our legends here in the south." Father Xavier exclaimed with a smile across his thin lips.

"Philosophy has many interests and the belief of the ancients is a fascinating subject in its own right." I replied.

"That is very true, my son." replied the Padre. "Whilst my ancestry is partly European and I am a man of God, I have found that there is room in our theology for the beliefs of the local people. You will see our mermaids carved on the façade of the cathedral at Puno in the Plaza de Armas[2]. The people may come to our churches to say Mass

---

[2] The Plaza de Armas ("Arms Square") is the major plaza in the city similar to other South American cities. On some recent maps it is called the Plaza Mayor de Puno ("Main Square of Puno")

but they will still burn a llama foetus as a sacrifice to the apu[3] of the mountain before taking their herds to summer pastures."

"That is very important to these simple people who have been able to accommodate the old beliefs into Christianity, so who are we to put them to ridicule?" I replied.

"Again, that is also true. You are indeed a philosopher but I suspect that you know more about the common people than a cloistered academic! You have the height and thin face of a European but the high cheekbones of the Andino. Señor Pablo here if I may continue my humble observations, is a true Andino." Padre Xavier said with his enigmatic smile and sideways glance.

"You are very perceptive, Padre" I replied, "as you have deduced, I am a mestizo and my

---

[3] Apu – the god attributed to particular mountains in the high Andes.

mother's family can be traced back to Incan nobility. Pablo, here is of the Quechua-speaking people who live in northern Peru although he now resides in Cuzco".

"That is true, Padre." said Garcia with a huge grin; no longer the humble manservant but the upright ex-soldier.

"Imanallatac canqui?[4]" asked Father Xavier in Quechua.

"Allillanmi[5]" Garcia replied without thinking, using the Runasimi or Cuzco dialect of Quechua, then looked at me with some apprehension.

[4] Imanallatac canqui? ("EE-mah-nah-YA-tahk CAHNG-ee.") Quechua of Ecuador for a generalised term of informal greeting loosely translated to "How are you" but showing some pleasure in the meeting.
[5] Allillanmi (AYI -yanmi) – "I'm fine." in Quechua of the south.

"Ah! I see that you have the Quechua language, a northern dialect, perhaps from Ecuador, Padre." I replied smiling.

"You are a man of constant surprises, Don Hernán. You are indeed a scholar." Father Xavier replied with a wide smile. "You too have the Runasimi[6] of the old people, I would assume?"

"Yes, Father, as I have said, I have Incan heritage on my mother's side, but where did you learn the language?" I asked.

Father Xavier laughed and spread his arms out in a manner of depreciation. "It is merely a matter of birth that I have all of the outward features which you may associate with a creole[7] – but I too have Andean antecedents and learnt the Runasimi at home; but then I have many languages."

[6] How the Quechua-speaking peoples referred to their language.
[7] Creole – term often used in Spanish Americas for a local born of purely European, usually Spanish blood.

"And so, Padre, where did you call home if I may be so bold as to ask?" I enquired.

The old priest spread out his arms and with a smile said: "Where do Jesuits call home? Why, Don Hernán, we have the whole world as our home, free to roam and bring the word of God to those who would receive it," he said with a smile. "As you have guessed, I was born and raised here in Peru, but have spent much time in the mountains of Ecuador where I became familiar with the local dialect. For the present, I will reside briefly in Puno where I have the task of giving some advice and encouragement to my infirmed brother, Father Ignatius at the Church of Saint John the Baptist. Soon he will start preparations for our Fiesta de la Virgen de la Candelaria[8] in the New Year. This is when the statue of the Virgin, the patroness of the city, is paraded from our church where she lives to the Cathedral in the

[8] Festival of the Virgin of the Candles.

Plaza de Armas. Have you been to Puno, my son?"

"For only a short time, Padre. I was there in 1882 only for but a brief few month. But alas I was very busy with my studies and did not have much time to explore the city."

"Ah yes! the Campaigns of the Sierra were being waged at that time here and further down the mountains as I recall. What were you then, Don Hernán a Capitán and perhaps now something grander; a Colonel perhaps?"

I laughed at the padre's perception which was too close to the truth for my own comfort. "Well, I was a Mayor in the Reserves, Padre when I last visited this area and did not really have time to explore the city at length as the Chileans had invaded and I needed to be elsewhere." I thought that it was expedient not to tell the good priest that it was here that I had met Garcia for the first time trying to hold the remnants of our southern forces together and spying on the enemy in the city.

"And you, Señor Pablo?" he said turning his smiling face towards Garcia, "may I assume that you were a non-commissioned officer; a Sargento perhaps?"

Garcia looked at me with some uncertainty and lowered his eyes as to hide his innocence. Father Xavier turn to me with a smile and said:

"It is of no importance and I am sorry to make so many assumptions about good men whom I have only just met. It is just my way and my training in the methods of scientific enquiry. You see that I have a great interest in my fellow man and it is the nature of us Jesuits to seek knowledge" Father Xavier continued with a deprecating spread of his open arms. "Those times are probably worth forgetting."

"They were a troubled time in the history of Peru, Padre. Many good men died and our country and poor Bolivia lost her coastline and suffered badly" I replied solemnly.

For a while there was nothing to be said, the silence was only broken by the jangle of the coach hardness and the noise of the wheels on the dusty highway. Outside, the panorama of the small farms nestled tightly in this narrow valley of the Altiplano passed slowly by. To our left, the mighty Urubamba River had slowed its mad rush from the snow-capped mountains further north and now flowed lazily along the small plain between the road and the barren hills. Soon these hills were covered in deep shadow as the sun slowly crept below the hills on the other side of the narrow valley.

It was almost nightfall when we crossed the small stone bridge which crossed the river and rattled into the small hamlet of Quiquijana and our stop for the night.

As the coach pulled into the courtyard of our staging post, Father Xavier again leaned over and said in almost a confidential tone:

"Here the Urubamba is called the Willkanuta River which is an Aymara term meaning 'the house of the Sun' for this river was sacred to the people and the mighty Urubamba is also called the 'sacred river' in Quechua."

"Yes," I replied, "it has many names in many local languages but it has always been a source of life in these mountains."

"In many ways, Don Hernán. There is a nearby peak here which is called 'Quri' which in the Quechua language means 'gold'; something which our Spanish ancestors would have had the greatest of interest."

Our stay in the nearby posada was a comfortable one despite the cold wind which blew down off the snow-capped peaks beyond the hills which surrounded the town. There was a good fire prepared in the inn's front room where the owner welcomed us with a substantial Seco Tajime[9] and freshly baked bread rolls. The evening quickly passed in these comfortable surroundings with cigars and a little wine. Garcia by now had relaxed and was more of his old self and spoke of his family and little farm in the hills above Cuzco. We all retired early as tomorrow would be a long journey.

The next day, we watched the loading of the coach and one of the local farmers climbed up onto the seats on the outside rear of the coach, positioning his large bundle most securely with cords. With a loud "¡vamonos!"[10] and a rattle of the reins, we again continued our journey south to Puno.

[9] Seco Tajime or Seco de Carne is a typical Peruvian stew of mutton with potatoes, pumpkin, peas, onions with garlic and cilantro (a herb similar to coriander).
[10] "Let's go!"

The three of us inside the coach had by now become good friends so the next leg of our dusty trip to the town of Sicuani passed very quickly. The town itself, when we arrived in the late afternoon, was a charming place and much more substantial than our last stop. It had a lovely, spacious Plaza de Armas with tall palms and some of the surrounding buildings had white and blue terraces which were quite attractive in the evening light.

In the morning, our new coachman advised us that we should take extra provisions for the next leg of our trip would be a very long one to our next overnight stop at Ayaviri some hundred kilometres to our south. There would be some brief stops along the way and a change in drivers and horses at Santa Rosa but it would be a long while before we would have a comfortable bed. Again, we set off with our coachman urging his horses on and his assistant clinging to his seat and waving to the children who ran alongside the horses cheering us on our way.

The next part of our journey was the longest and most difficult, but Father Xavier was true to his word and made no more deductions about Garcia and I nor did he elaborate on his own life, save for his rich knowledge of local customs and stories. There was a brief stop at the Abra La Raya[11] to spell the horses and an opportunity for us to buy some trinkets from the many small stalls of local women who had come from local villages to sell their handicrafts to travellers on the road. From La Raya, the road wound its way out of the narrow valley of the Urubamba River where the land became flatter and the valley wider as we approached the true Altiplano which held the immense expanse of Lake Titicaca. Tomorrow we would travel out onto this plain, but tonight we would stay at Ayaviri,

[11] "The border pass" at 4350 m above sea level, it marks the border between the Cuzco and Puno regions where the valley opens out into the true Altiplano.

Sexta Historia: La Confesión del Sacerdote
(Sixth Story: The Priest's Confession

Our last day of our journey to Puno and into territory of past memories. We were now in the low hills north of the lake and approaching the village of Pucara. Garcia was looking out of the window and showed some excitement.

"Look, Patrón!" he cried pointing out towards a distant hill with a prominent layer of rock running down its side at a steep angle, "there is the tilted rock of our first meeting."

I quickly shook my head and quickly brought my fingers up to my lips. In his excitement he had forgotten our new guises but a quick look at our other companion gave me some reassurance that our secrets were still safe for Father Xavier had dozed off and had his head now resting on his chest, his Bible on his lap still open at his morning reading.

Indeed, Garcia had good cause to be excited for it was in these very hills that we had first met those many years ago. I had brought a small military force consisting of those Headquarters staff who were usually considered non-combatants south to help defend our country from the invasion of units of the Chilean army during the War of the Pacific. I had found Garcia, then a Sargento Primero[1], attempting to reorganise the remnants of our army and the local militia who had escaped the Chilean invasion and were then regrouping in these hills.

"These are dangerous hills." Father Xavier quietly remarked, raising his head and closing his Bible, "there are still groups of men here who continued the war on long after the treaty was signed. Some say that many have turned to banditry but who can say whether they still watch for the southern

[1] Sargento Primero - Sergeant

invaders or fight for the local people against the wealthy Hacendados[2] here about."

"Yes, I have heard that the local people formed militia and found very courageously against the invaders, both here and further down the mountains to Arequipa." I replied, knowing full well from my own personal experiences here in these very hills that the people had responded rapidly to the government's call to arms regardless that they were still denied land reforms and were still exploited even after the end of the war.

Perhaps there had been some anticipation of feeling of foreboding in Father Xavier's comments for it was not any more than an hour later that the coach slowed down as it rounded a sharp bend. I looked out from the window and saw that a line of large rocks had been placed across the road; a

[2] Owners of large Haciendas or estates who often exploited local people as indentured farm laborers.

silent line of local farmers dressed in their usual chullos[3], pantaloons, sandals and striped ponchos.

Father Xavier looked out and smiled. "It looks like some of the local farmers are protesting again. It is nothing, really. There are some disputes against the acquisition of some land for the new railway which the British are building from Puno, but usually the matters are resolved."

The coach driver and his assistant had both climbed down from their seats and were talking with one of the farmers. This barrier was not uncommon and the farmers knew that the owners of the coach line were also a victim of the new technology. What was not common was the small group of men who emerged from behind a large boulder and approached the coach. The farmers moved away from their small barricade and then walked off slowly down the hill.

[3] Chullos are woven caps with ear flaps and tassels often worn by men in the Andes.

"This does not look good, Patrón!" said Garcia, opening his coat and loosening his knife inside its hidden scabbard. I had left my waistcoat and my pistol in my travelling bag thinking that our journey would be a peaceful one. At least I still had my knife in my boot.

"All of you inside, get out!" cried one of the men who now came up to the coach and flung open the door.

Father Xavier climbed out of coach and Garcia and I followed. The men motioned us to move over with the two coachmen who were now standing a little way from the coach and looking afraid.

It was then that their leader came closer to the coach. He was a well-built man although of an average height for the local Andinos with a typically broad chest and strong limbs. Unlike his companions he did not have a bandana covering his face which was a deep brown typical of many farmers who had spent most of their lives out in the sun. 'The sons of Inti' my mother would call such people who had these darker complexions. She had no European blood but her skin was lighter in colour denoting her noble ancestry so that she always went covered when out in the sun.

The leader also set himself apart from his followers by his dress. The others wore the usual dress of local farmers of homespun pantaloons and ponchos with either chullos or broad cloth sombreros for head covering and sandals on their feet. Their leader also wore a broad-brimmed sombrero but also wore a faded blue army coat over his pantaloons and also, he wore brown leather boots. There were bright patches on the upper sleeve of his tunic showing that he had once been a Sargento Primera. His broad face was a hard one; that of a man who had seen some of the worst of life and I deduced from his general appearance that he may have been a deserter at the end of the war and now made his living as a bandit. He approached us with some menace.

Suddenly he became startled and stood more erect, his hands by his sides and his mouth partly open below his thin black moustaches.

"Padre…. I am sorry." He stammered looking at Father Xavier who now stepped in front of our pitiful little group.

"It is well, my son" he said putting his arm around the shoulder of the bandit leader and walking him a little way off from us and the bandit's men. They stood apart for a while, the priest and the bandit, whose head was now bowed like a little child being consoled by his parent. Father Xavier spoke in a low voice and so his words were inaudible to us. Eventually he made the sign of the cross over the bandit who also crossed himself and gave a slight bow to God or Father Xavier, I knew not to whom.

Father Xavier returned to our group with his usual enigmatic smile and a wave of dismissal.

"Come! Let us now resume our journey, for the rocks will be cleared by these good people who have seen the folly of their ways."

This was a surprising and most happy event. Garcia pushed his wicked knife deeper into his shoulder holster and I returned my hand from the side of my boot. We climbed back into the coach and soon the drivers had us on our way.

"You indeed have a way with God's word." I said to the priest once we had settled into our seats.

"Yes, my son," he replied with a smile, "they are like little children and have their own view of the world. It is just a matter of showing them that the truth of God's mercy is for all of us and not just for the wealthy."

No more was said for a while; however, my curiosity and suspicions had been raised. Father Xavier and the bandit leader seemed to be much more friendly than a simple priest counselling a miscreant on the errors of his ways. Garcia, too was uneasy for he now looked at the priest with than intensity that Andinos have when they are troubled. I could not hold back so I turned to Father Xavier and said: "You seemed to be on excellent terms with our bandit friend, back there, Father?"

The old priest looked up with some sadness in his eyes and replied. "Perhaps it is time for confession, my son. It is difficult sometimes to hide the scars of the past and you seem to be a man of intuition from whom deception is easily discovered." He sat back and straightened his shoulders and the enigmatic smile returned to his face. "So then, I will tell you my story:

You were correct in assuming that I had been acquainted with that fellow Don Hernán...his name is Roberto by the way…and he is well-respected in this part of the country except by the local police of course; some of whom see him as a bandit. You are also correct in assuming that I have had some military training. You see I came from a military family; my father was a Colonel and fought in the battle of Ayacucho[4] under the liberator General Antonio José de Sucre y Alcalá. My grandfather had been in the Spanish Army but married a girl from the Aymara nobility; her people still live in this very district in Juliaca[5], a city we will pass through shortly. Naturally, it was expected that I too should follow the family tradition, so without much ceremony I was sent to the Military Institute which later became the Military School at Chorrillos near Lima. You know of it, Don Hernán?"

[4] Battle of Ayacucho took place on 9th December 1824, near the city of that name in Peru about 200 km southeast of Lima. It marked the beginning of Peruvian independence.
[5] Juliaca – pronounced HOOLI -AKA is the biggest city on Lake Titicaca and because of the expanse of flat land has the regional airport.

"Certainly, Father. It is the most prestigious Officer Training institution." I replied, having attended Reserve training there myself, "but please go on; I am curious as to why a soldier would become a man of God."

"Ha!" Father Xavier laughed. "You forget that I am a Jesuit so why should not a soldier follow in the footsteps of our gracious founder Saint Ignatius de Loyola who was also a soldier? Well...to answer your question; I graduated as an Ensign[6] in the cavalry and began my illustrious military career in and around Lima, most of it in the Headquarters thanks to my father's influence. Without boring you with the details, I was eventually posted to the Juliaca region in 1867 as a Capitán de Tropa[7]. You will see the city of Juliaca soon by the way, for it is on this very road."

[6] Now Second Lieutenant – the lowest officer rank
[7] Troop Captain – in charge of a troop of cavalry, about 100 men.

"Yes, I know of Juliaca." I replied. Garcia and I had sometimes sent scouts into the city and further south looking for Chilean units during the war, but I did not wish Father Xavier to know of this fact. "It is one of our country's major trading centres. I believe that its name comes from the Quechua term 'Xullaskca kaipi'[8], does it not?"

Father Xavier's enigmatic smile returned, "Your Quechua and geography are excellent Don Hernán, as you probably know it refers to the state of the weather when the Incas arrived there. It was drizzling with rain then, but today we simply call it La Ciudad Ventosa[9].

"Now Father, please continue. I am interested to hear about your conversion from Ensign to Jesuit?"

---

[8] Quechua – "It has drizzled" referring to the state of the local hills when the Inca army arrived in that location.
[9] Spanish: 'The Windy City'.

"Well, my son that is part of my life which I usually choose to forget. But you are a man of understanding so I will give you but a brief account. You may recall from our history that there had been some trouble in the Puno district and to the north of the lake. The powerful landowners of the region had got rich in the wool trade with the British but at the expense of the local people who were used on the great haciendas as virtual slaves. Consequently, the poor people staged a revolt which was complicated by some local political agitation against the government. It was in January of the next year that my troop of Hussars where dispatched to the village of Huancané some forty kilometres to our northeast around the edge of the lake. We had been called out in support of other units and the militia who had been sent to supress the local population.

In the years before this revolt, a prominent merchant and rich landowner, Juan Bustamante who had also been a former elected Prefect of the district of Puno, became the champion and representative of the local indigenous people. At the request of the other landowners in the region, the government sent an army under the command of General Baltazar Caravedo, to subdue the indigenous people. But Caravedo refused to do this as he preferred dialogue. In Huancané, Bustamante reached an agreement with General Caravedo, who withdrew with his troops to Lima. The landowners accused Caravedo of complicity with the indigenous people and promoted a revolt against the government of President Prado and again hostilities broke out with the involvement of the indigenous people. So, again we were called out in support of the government.

It was too late! By the time I arrived with my troop, many old scores had been settled, the people once more suppressed and their leader, Juan Bustamante had been killed. Some say that he had been very badly treated then hung by his heels and decapitated. I was very personally shocked by his death as my Grandmother was of the same people who now were once more being mistreated and their just cause for land and freedom had been again dashed."

"I understand, Father" I said with some sadness." I had been a young student at the time and had read some of Señor Bustamante's books and followed his writings in the newspaper *El Comercio*."

"Yes, Bustamante was truly an intellectual of the first order and a friend of the common people. His death was a sad blow for the rights of the indigenous peoples. Their suppression was abhorrent to me so I resigned my commission and returned to Lima. My father was horrified and would not listen to my reasons, even if it was the very people of his own mother who were being suppressed. Because of this ill-feeling, I left Peru and went north into Ecuador where the political side of my life would be of little consequence. After a year of menial jobs and considerable self-evaluation I joined the Society of Jesus. So that is my story, Don Hernán; you have now heard my full confession," he said with a depreciating laugh. "So, what now is my penitence?"

I looked directly into his eyes and replied "You have already done your penitence, good father. You do not need my absolution for we all have our own sins of which only God can forgive."

There was silence for some time and the coach rattled on towards Juliaca and Puno beyond.

It was almost dusk when our couch pulled into the Coaching Station on the shores of the Lake Titicaca. There were several coaches waiting to depart and so there was the usual crowd of people: well-dressed merchants in their European attire and valises; local people in a variety of village costumes with their bundles carried over their shoulders; and the many ostlers and servants loading and unloading baggage.

Our bags had been handed down from on top of the coach as we said our farewell to Father Xavier. I watched him as he strode purposely into the crowd and it was then that he did something unexpected and rather unsettling to my new complacency. He turned, made the sign of the cross as a form of a benediction and with his usual enigmatic smile called out:

"Ve con Dios[10], Colonel!" and he sharply turned and melted into the crowd.

[10] "Go with God" or "Godspeed" a typical Spanish farewell.

Séptima Historia: de Pumas y Ranas
(Seventh Story: of Pumas and Frogs)

The benediction of Father Xavier had rattled my composure; did he guess of my true rank or did he know more than I had supposed? He was indeed a mystery.

Garcia and I hired a small donkey trap and found our posada on the Avenida La Torre, only a few blocks away. It was dark by then so we appreciated the cheerful lights of the posada's courtyard as well as the welcome by its owner, Señor Braulio an open and friendly man who seemed to have a solution to every problem.

The next day, I made arrangements to visit the Head of the Philosophy Department at the Universidad de Puno; my cover excuse for making the journey to Puno. Garcia had decided to visit the well-known and popular Mercado de

Contrabando[1] at the water front. Señor Braulio had told him about these markets over many glasses of cerveza[2] the previous night so he was interested in seeing what small items he could buy having the extra excitement that they were illegal goods. Soldiers are like that.

These markets were extensive and sold about everything imaginable from food items to the latest household items. There had always been an active trading network across Lake Titicaca from one side to the other; well before the Incas and then the Spaniards arrived. The Spaniards had carved up the country into their many and separate governmental regions with little regard to the tribal boundaries of the indigenous people. The border between southern Peru and Bolivia was arbitrarily drawn down through Lake Titicaca. But the trading network across the lake continued. To be sure, both counties maintained small naval units to control smuggling, but the

[1] Contraband market where smuggled goods are sold.
[2] Beer

outcome was never in doubt. It would be hard for Customs Officers to arrest people who were their relatives and perhaps they too also gained from some trade. Whenever government officials arrived from Lima or Cuzco, there naturally would be some arrests. Juan, or Pedro or Antonio would be seized and locked up for the duration of the official's inspection and then released thereafter. The Mercado de Contrabando thrived, especially with woollen goods made in the homes of both countries.

For my part, I walked down towards the lake and to the Universidad de Puno to pay my respects to the Head of Philosophy there.

Professor Guillermo Menendez Rojas was a rotund, gregarious man of about fifty years of age. He greeted me with a firm handshake and a broad smile.

"Welcome to Puno, Doctor Moreno. I hope that you would stay a while with us. I have read some of your papers and I am interested in your work on the soldier-philosophers of ancient Greece."

"Thank you, Don Guillermo, but alas my visit will be but a short one. I am continuing my journey to La Paz where I also have some research tasks," I lied.

"Well in that case, Doctor Moreno, allow me to show you a little of our city. Come! I hope that you do not mind walking as that is the best way to see our city?"

With that he picked up his hat from his desk and walked briskly out of his study. I followed as fast as I could to keep up with his fast past.

We walked around the edge of the lake along the Avenida Costanera with its open park on one side and the broad waters of Lake Titicaca on the other. The buildings along this avenue were the usual adobe structures of two or three storeys and seemed to be occupied by traders in the most part. We turned into a broad street, the Calle Los Incas, which led into the heart of the city.

The people who went about their daily tasks seemed healthy enough; some in modern European dress, others in local costumes and others in a colourful mixture of both. The dress was usually sober in the main with men in trousers, shirts and sandals and the ladies in long skirts and colourful lliclas[3] and a variety of head wear denoting their village of origin; the small bowler hats, recently imported for the railway workers were most common.

We crossed several main streets and then continued walking along to where the Calle Los Incas suddenly narrowed until it opened into a small plaza. To our right was an impressive stone building painted blue with white simulated

---

[3] Llicllas (pronounced Yeek-ya) – The *lliclla* or *manta* is a colourful cape worn by Quechua women, woven in the shape of a square and worn across the back and shoulders like a miniature shawl.

colonnades and white balconies on its line of windows.

"You like it?" asked the professor seeing my interest.

"Yes, it is a most impressive building" I replied.

"It is the Glorioso Colegio Nacional de San Carlos[4] and it was founded in 1828 by the great liberator Simon Bolivar himself. It is one of our most prestigious educational institutions here, dedicated to our young people. Its' most famous son was Manuel Pino who was also a teacher of philosophy here. During the war with the Chileans, he and his students fought them when this very square was made into one of the Chilean's barracks. Unfortunately, he later died at

[4] Glorious National College of Saint Charles. Saint Charles or San Carlos, was Charles Borromeo (Italian:1538 – 1584) was the Latin archbishop of Milan and a cardinal of the Catholic Church who carried out many reforms.

the Battle of Miraflores[5]. The good citizens of Puno have plans to name this square after him and to build a statue in his honour. Were you in the war, Doctor Morano?" he asked.

"I was just a Reservist." I replied. "No great battles for me, I am afraid."

"Well, then. Let us not talk of such sad events. Here is the Church of San Juan Bautista," he said, pointing to a lovely church opposite the college. It had three frontal spires and was painted in white, yellow and grey.

"It has recently been rebuilt on the site of the old chapel which probably predated the founding of this city in 1668. It is a small but very important church because it holds the statue of the Virgen of Candelaria - the patron saint of Puno".

---

[5] The Battle of Miraflores occurred on January 15, 1881 in the Miraflores District of Lima.

I felt the urge to go in and ask for my former travelling companion Father Xavier, but perhaps another time. Professor Menendez quickly walked off, turning into a narrow, cobbled street which contained many small shops huddled together in the usual style and usually of two-storey adobe brick with red tiled rooves. Soon we entered the main plaza.

"Here is our Plaza de Armas and you can see the usual government buildings, the police barracks, and of course our beautiful cathedral, the Catedral Basílica San Carlos Borromeo. It was built in the Andean Baroque style and finished in 1747. Let's push on, you must visit the cathedral before you leave."

We walked past the ordered stone walls of the cathedral and along the Jirón[6] Deustua which suddenly became very steep as we climbed up into the side of the wide amphitheatre which

[6] Jirón – a small, narrow street as named.

holds the city against the wide stretch of the blue Lake Titicaca.

It was a very difficult climb, even for one used to the high altitude of the Altiplano, but eventually we reached a small, flat rocky knoll upon which was built a wide stone plinth in the Incan style showing a broad, square face. Surmounting this was a stature of an Inca dressed in the traditional kilt and robe of a chief. His stern face looking out towards the lake.

"This is the Cerrito Huajsapata[7] and the statue is of Manco Cápac, the founder of the Inca Empire. It is said that he and his family were born from an island in the lake, the children of Inti the god of the Sun. But I am sure that you know that story well?" he said with a knowing look.

---

[7] Cerrito = *little hill* and the indigenous word '*Huajsapata*' pronounced *hhrrr sapata* and is often given a meaning of 'witness of my love' so it probably refers to the love of the Lake and the land by the Inca Manco Cápac or simply a 'lovers' hill' with a beautiful view of the lake.

"Indeed," I answered with a smile. "My mother, whose ancestors were of the Incan nobility of Cuzco often told me the story"

"Ah! But did you know that there are supposed to be great caves and tunnels under this hill which reach all the way to the temple of the Sun[8] in your fair city?"

"No!" I laughed, "that is one story which my mother neglected to tell me. Perhaps one day we could find them and use them as a fast way of travelling between the two cities."

He turned and faced the vast extent of the lake which stretched out before us beyond the terracotta rooves of the city. It was a fine day and I could see the distant hills stretching out on

[8] *Templo de Koricancha* - '*The Golden Temple*', from the Quechua *quri* gold and *kancha* enclosure also called the Temple of the Sun was the original Incan temple in Cuzco dedicated to Inti the sun. The Convent of Santo Domingo, the monastery of the Dominicans was built upon it in 1680.

either side of the blue waters of the lake, merging with the sky and white clouds in the distance.

"You see that knoll higher up on the surrounding ridge?" the professor continued. "That is called the Mirador Puma Uta[9] and from there we would get a much better understanding of the immensity of this great lake. It is said that the name of the lake comes from the local Aymara word 'titiq'aq'a' which loosely translates as the 'grey puma'. There is much debate about this and why the name should refer to our wild cat. Some say this refers to an ancient carving of a puma on the side of the sacred island of Isla del Sol out there on the lake but others say that it refers to the very shape of the lake itself which looks like a hunting puma. The Incas believed the puma, condor and the snake to be sacred because of its respective strength, ability to fly and its speed. But who knows?"

[9] The lookout of the sacred Puma.

I looked out again at the sparkling blue waters of this, the highest of deep freshwater lakes and imagined how the ancient inhabitants could imagine the shape of this lake as a great puma as seen from above, but then I remembered the stone outlines of animals on the coastal plain of Nazca well to our north. It was well within the mathematical and surveying knowledge of these ancient people to visualise a surface feature from above.

"There is another local story about the lake and another one of its creatures which I find fascinating." the professor said. He sat down on the rock with his back against the statue's plinth and wiped his brow with an old handkerchief. "Would you like to hear it?"

"To be sure, Professor, I know little of the local stories hereabouts, as my people came from Cuzco well after the Incas settled there." I replied, joining the old man on sharp, grey stone.

"Good! Well then, let me begin" he said as he straightened out his shirt front much like I imagined he would do at the start of one of his lectures at the university.

"It is a story of a toad," he laughed, "or more correctly, a frog. *Telmatobius culeus*, to be exact; commonly known as the Titicaca water frog. It is a medium to large frog which inhabits the lake but is becoming very scarce in recent times. It is said that they once occurred here in very large numbers and that they inhabited a fabulous city beneath the lake. The story goes on to say that one night, when the Incan army of Túpac Yupanqui[10] arrived at the lake not far from the sacred site of Puma Uta, one of the night sentries encountered a beautiful woman dressed in a wide, flowing green robe and having large, golden eyes which spoke to him of love. He became bewitched by her and fell into a happy, deep sleep. When he was awoken by the relieving guard, he was ashamed

---

[10] Túpac Yupanqui 1441–c. 1493, the son of Pachacuti, was the tenth Inca of the Inca Empire and his son was Huayna Capac.

and told him about the beautiful young maiden with the golden eyes. Alarmed at this, the rest of the guard was called out and the men searched the totora reeds around the shores of the lake. There they encountered this beautiful maiden with the golden eyes. When they pursued her, she was suddenly transformed into a giant frog with golden eyes and taking one last look at the men, dived into the smooth, dark waters of the lake. When the Inca[11] heard of this, he had his men cast great nets into the water. When they hauled them in, they were full of a great number of frogs led by two of great size with green skin and large golden eyes. In front of the Inca, the two great frogs turned into the beautiful woman and her equally handsome consort. They gave the Inca a haughty glance and then returned to their natural shape, leading their companions out of the lake and up into the hills beyond the astonished soldiers. Inti the Sun had just appeared over the mountains to the east and seeing the plight of frogs who were

[11] The term 'Inca' refers to the emperor here as well as to his people.

now in danger from the spears of the soldiers, turned them into the large stones you can see not far from here."

I looked up into the ridge of the Puma Uta just above us which were strewn with large stones and imagined a group of frogs fleeing from the spears of the Incan soldiers.

"Furthermore" continued the professor, "it is said that some of the locals still believe that there is a mysterious city beneath the lake. Furthermore, should you go to the shore at midnight and encounter one of its inhabitants, they will offer you ears of corn made of gold for the return of their king and queen. A fascinating story is it not?"

"Yes indeed, Professor. The lake certainly looks as though it would contain great mystery and it is interesting how all local peoples have tales which explain their natural surroundings."

My thoughts were suddenly interrupted when my eye caught a smudge of faint black smoke well out upon the water.

"Professor, there is a steamer out on the lake!" I exclaimed.

"You have good eyes, Doctor Moreno, that is indeed a steamer. It is our *Yavari* which is both a gunboat for our navy and a cargo boat which carries passengers across the lake. It was named after the Yavary[12] River, a tributary of the Amazon on our north eastern border with Brazil"

"But where was it built?" I enquired, "I know of no shipyard anywhere near the lake!"

"Ah, that is the beauty of our industrial age, Doctor Moreno. The *Yavari* was built in an ironworks in London in 1861 and then broken down into small pieces which could be

---

[12] Also called the Javary River.

reassembled. It was shipped out to Arica on what was once the coast of Bolivia, then by railway to Tacna and then on the backs of poor mules up the mountain roads to the lake where it was reassemble. Quite a feat of engineering, yes?"

"That is a remarkable story, Professor, but where does the Yavari get its fuel; its coal, its timber?"

"Ah. Yes, more of the adaptability and common sense of Peru! The Yavari is able to use dried llama dung as its fuel. We are an ingenious people and there are plenty of llamas here in the Altiplano." He said, tapping the side of his nose with his finger. "It combines the unusual functions of a gunboat, a passenger ship and of course a trading vessel – but I doubt that there is much use for it as a gunboat. We are usually on good terms with our Bolivian neighbours across the lake and the smuggling trade between the two countries is almost an acceptable occupation. The local people were trading across the lake for centuries before the Spaniards decided to draw a border line down its middle."

I looked out across the broad, blue waters of the lake and the hills beyond. There was a momentary flash of light closer into the city on a broad expanse of yellow floating on the water.

"What is over there?" I asked and pointed in the direction of the expanse of yellow.

"Ha!" said the professor, "you have found the home of the Uru[13] who live on the floating islands made from tied bundles of the totora reed found in abundance around the lake. It is said that they fled to the lake to escape invaders. Perhaps the Aymara who live here and certainly the Incas and Spaniards who came later. They build beautiful boats of reed bundles and live in comfortable reed thatched houses on their many islands. Of course, they are now very much assimilated with the

---

[13] Uru or Los Uros (*Qhas Qut suñi* in the old Uru language).

mainland peoples but many still prefer their island homes with their own way of life."

"How do they make a living?" I asked, "fishing perhaps?"

"Oh, yes. They are good fishermen and they make small fish pens by cutting a large square hole in their islands which they then line with nets. They catch the fish from the lake and then put them into their pens where they breed them and have fish whenever they want. Clever? No?"

"They would seem to have a good life then?" I replied.

"Well, most of the time. Their fears of the mainlanders have long since disappeared as has their language and customs and many have moved ashore over time. There is one interesting family tradition which remains when they have to maintain peace and harmony."

"Yes, what is that?" I asked.

"Well, now! if one member of the family has a major falling out or has dishonoured the family group, they simply cut off the part of the island occupied by the offender home with the large saws they use to shape their island. The offender is allowed to drift away from the family group to start a new life. Of course, should a new member join the family, it is an easy task to weave more reeds together and form a new part of the island for more living space."

The professor continued his description of the sights and history of the city of Puno. He was very proud of the city and of its potential for the future.

"There has been a great variation in the fortunes of Puno, especially with the demise of the silver mines to the east and the slump in the alpaca wool trade caused by the recent war[14], but we have the railway to Arequipa and beyond to the coast, so trade is beginning to return."

With that comment, he turned and made his way down the sharp limestone rocks of the Cerrito. I followed and we walked back down the hill and into the street which ran next to the eastern side of the cathedral. We stopped at a small, rectangular archway with a tiled roof next to a neat, two-storeyed building painted in a bright yellow colour. A small sign on the wall next to the archway read 'Café Bar' where the professor bade me enter.

Through the archway was a small but delightful tiled courtyard filled with a variety of flowering cactus plants and wooden seats and tables. Beyond was the welcoming interior of the café.

[14] The War of the Pacific – Bolivia lost its coastal strip and important trade routes for Peru and Bolivia to coastal centres which now form part of Chile.

"Time for a good coffee, if you would like one, Doctor Moreno, or perhaps something more traditional such as Mate de Coca[15] should you need it" he said with a sideways glance and a smile.

I laughed at that suggestion. "Thank you, all the same, but as a native of Cuzco I know the use of coca very well and I am well at home at this altitude."

"Perhaps it is not too early for you to try our local drink in honour of the hill we have just climbed – the *Huajsapata*[16]. It is a hot mulled wine which you can only find here in Puno. Too much of it in our cold winter at this altitude will give you altitude sickness even if you are an Andino," he laughed as we entered the café. "Come! Let us have a good

---

[15] An herbal tea made by infusing leaves of the coca plant in boiling water. Very useful for altitude sickness.
[16] This is a hot mulled wine mixed with grenadine, orange bitters and spices served with a slice of orange. Pisco, a form of Peruvian brandy is a much better substitute for the wine.

coffee and then I will show you our beautiful cathedral before I let you go in our faculty library."

Octava Historia: Pecadores y Santos
(Eighth Story: Sinners and Saints)

The next day was a beautiful one, so Garcia and I decided to walk to the coach station down near the waterfront. We had travelled light and so this would be no problem as we were both used to our former military baggage. We ate our simple breakfast of warm bread rolls, fruit and mate de coco, paid our dues before saying farewell to our genial host, Señor Braulio and heading off down Avenida La Torre with the sun coming up over the low hills beyond the lake before us. We turned into the Calle Los Incas as we walked towards the waterfront. The early morning bustle was just beginning with street sellers offering freshly cooked corn to the good people of Puno heading off to work. A tricycle rickshaw driver offered to carry us for his usual small fee, so we accepted. Down the avenida we went at a good pace, dodging the many small hand-drawn and donkey-drawn carts which carried a variety of fruits and vegetables and other goods to the morning markets.

Garcia opened his leather satchel and showed me the small items which he had purchased at the Mercado de Contrabando; a few delightful little toys for his children, a hand-embroidered blouse for his wife and a set of three small throwing-knives set in a leather pouch.

"One should always be prepared!" he offered his explanation for this item with a shrug of his shoulders.

I had thought that we had already made that provision, for the thought of passing our small bags through Bolivian Customs later that day meant that we carried our various arms concealed about our bodies.

We turned into the appropriately named Avenida Simon Bolivar and soon arrived at the Coaching Station. We had a short wait whilst I validated our tickets and made arrangements for our bags to be put on top of the coach. To me, waiting for a coach always seemed to be one of expectation mixed with some excitement. Here, in Puno it was no different; the other passengers having their friends and relatives bidding them farewell simply added to the effect.

Our coach was more brightly painted than the sombre Four-in-hand which had conveyed us from Cuzco. When the driver loudly announced that we should be leaving soon, I noticed that today, our coach would probably have a full load.

The assistant took our tickets, gave them a quick inspection and with a toothless smile directed us to the cab with an open hand. I noticed that there already were a number of local people clambering up onto the open seats at the rear of the cab lifting up an assortment of baskets or carrying bundles in their striped woven shoulder cloths or llikllas. These were simple people with simple tasks;

going back home perhaps, or to sell or trade their few items along the journey.

Garcia and I climbed up into the coach's cab along with the other passengers. We had once again assumed to disguise of the academic traveller, Doctor Hernán Vázquez and his assistant Pablo. Today we were joined by four other passengers so that the cab was full and there was little space for comfort. Luckily the distance to our destination at Copacabana in Bolivia was only a day's journey. We all adjusted ourselves to the discomfort of our surroundings as the coach lurched off with the customary "¡vamonos!"

Our travelling companions seemed to be a mixed assortment; a young man of Andino descent dressed in his best European clothes, a rather gaunt man of middle age who had the stern and fussy appearance of an undertaker on business and a couple of middle age and rotund appearance whom, from their earlier loud complaints about the crowded nature of the coaching station and their florid appearance suggested that they were from England. It would be an interesting journey.

My assumptions about the couple proved to be correct. Almost as soon as we had left the coaching station and turned into the broad expanse of the Avenida Simon Bolivar, the rotund and over dressed man thrust his hand out to the gaunt man whom I had dubbed 'the undertaker' and said with a loud but cheerful voice: "Charlie's tha name and buyin' wool's me game!"

The Undertaker looked up and said in a very clipped and precise low voice: "No hablo Ingles, señor"[1]. It was obvious that he did not want to be involved in any conversation and having given his response to the Englishman's overture, he turned and looked out of the window of the coach.

[1] "I do not speak English, Sir.

The rotund Englishman looked downcast and muttered as an apology "Oh...sorry. Me Español is mucho pocito"[2].

Not to be put off, he searched in some of the side pockets of his rather stretched waistcoat and produced a small wad of business cards which he proceeded to hand out to Garcia, to me and finally he stretched around the large expanse of his equally rotund wife to hand one to the young man sitting next to her at the other window.

I replied in English, "thank you, sir" and looked at his card.

'**Charles S. Cholmondeley, Esq**.
Purchaser of Fine Textiles
Elysium Mills,
Macclesfield, Cheshire, Great Britain.'

---

[2] This is a very poor attempt at speaking Spanish! What he meant to say was "Lo siento, mi Español es muy poco" for "my Spanish is very Little". A more appropriate reply would have been "Lo siento, solo hablo un poquito de español" for "I am sorry, I only speak a Little Spanish."

I gave him a nod of my head and a smile and replied in English: "My pleasure, Mister Cholmunderly"

"It's pronounced 'Chumley' – me name, that is," he responded with a depreciating grin which showed several gold teeth. "Nice to meet ya too, sinyour. It's good to 'ear me native tongue again. We've been travellin' up frum tha coast where we 'ave an agent in Arequipa and we're goin' on to La Paz to look for more trade. Wool…ya understand! Your alparka[3] wool is far better what we can grow on sheep back 'ome." He turned and with a pudgy hand indicated his equally rotund wife who sat in her many dresses and old-fashioned bonnet in the middle of the bench seat. She had a silk handkerchief placed over her mouth and nose and the slight smell of lavender had filled the coach. "This is me good lady wife, Mrs. Cholmondeley. She doesn't speak any of

[3] Some incorrect pronunciations here: "Llama" is pronounced like "Yama", the "ll' is sounded like a "y". Alpaca is better pronounced with a short "a" not the long "aa" as in "ark".

your lingo and finds the air a mite difficult to breath. Don't yer, Mother?"

The 'good lady wife' gave a sniff and a slight nod of her head in acknowledgement and returned to fumbling in her small bag of knitting which she had on her lap in order to refrain from any conversation.

"Perhaps Mister Chumley, I might suggest that you partake of some coca tea at our next stop. We call it 'mate de coca' here and you make it with coco leaves in hot water – very much like your English tea. It is very good for breathing if you are not used to our altitude. We are at almost four thousand metres above the sea and Europeans find it difficult in our thin air."

"Much gracias." He responded with an attempt to speak Spanish. He looked at Garcia hoping to engage him in conversation but before he did, I quickly interrupted him.

"This gentleman is Pablo, my assistant, and being a true man of these mountains does not speak any English; only Spanish and Quechua, the tongue of the Incas."

Garcia caught my English meaning and gave a faint smile to the Englishman and brought his finger up to his forehead in salute.

"Buen día, señor" he said with his usual broad smile, then looked down at the floor of the coach.

I explained to our new acquaintance that Garcia and I were travelling to Copacabana on some matters pertaining to my university and hoped that his journey further on to La Paz, the commercial hub of Bolivia, would be an advantageous and pleasant one.

The Englishman looked around the girth of his wife and asked the young man sitting at the window if he spoke English. He did this in his poor Spanish and the young man with a shy but friendly smile: "Lo siento pero no entiendo."[4]

I leaned over to him and with a smile repeated the question. The young man replied that he was sorry but he had no English and I gave his answer and apologies to the Englishman in his language.

"Well, then!" interrupted the Englishman, "Ya certainly 'ave great potential in yer country, Mister Vázquez. The wool trade 'as picked up remarkably well now that yer war is over. There's a ready market back 'ome, ya know! Aye! That there is! Yer people raise tha sheep and lamas and alparkas and we shippem 'ome to make fine textiles."

The Englishmen continued on with his discourse about English exploitation of the wool trade here in the southern regions of Peru and across the border into Bolivia. He complained about the

4 "I am sorry, but I do not understand"

opportunities missed in constructing the railways using English material and expertise; lamenting that the Americans had taken advantage of the country in building the railway from Arequipa and were now constructing the new line from Cuzco. He also complained about some of the wealthy landowners with whom he had to deal with. Men of wealth and of mixed European birth in the most part, who seem to have reverted to mere 'country bumpkins' as he called them.

I could not help but feel sorry for the local small land owners, shepherds and muleteers who had been displaced by these Gamonalismos[5] and the railway. It seemed that trade brought many sins and sinners upon the land in the name of prosperity.

[5] Gamonalismo - meaning "bossism," and derived from *gamonal*, a word meaning a "large landowner." It is often used when referring to the exploitation of the indigenous population, mainly by large landowners of European descent.

The Englishman continued his discourse about the trade advantages of being friendly to the British Empire, mostly directed to the roof of the carriage with his eyes closed. I had a brief and uncomfortable flashback in history and thought of the Incas arriving here in Puno with similar ideas. Eventually his discourse turned to snoring as he was rocked to sleep by the motion of the carriage.

I had noticed that the young man had brought out a small book which now sat closed on his lap.

"You are a student?" I ventured quietly.

"Yes, sir. I am, but I have travelling on to San Pablo de Tiquina to visit my uncle there. Do you know of it?"

"Only by my studies of local geography. It is where the coaches must be ferried across the narrow isthmus of the lake, is it not?" I replied.

"Yes, sir! that is correct. It is the narrow part of the lake between the main water and what the Bolivians call Lake Huinaymarca[6]. In Peru, we call it Lake Pequeño or the 'Little Lake.'"

"Thank you." I replied, taking out a small book which I had placed into my coat pocket. "My local almanac, which I purchased in Puno, suggests that the entirety of the lake resembles in shape a puma chasing a small rabbit. Perhaps this Lake Pequeño is the small rabbit, no?"

"Who can say, sir. I do not know much about such things." The student once more opened his own book and averted any further conversation.

Garcia had found the passing landscape much more interesting that our fellow passengers. We had left the closed-packed buildings and narrow cobbled streets and were now jingling along the dirt road which follows the lake around the large

[6] Sometimes written as 'Wiñaymarka Lake' which phonetically is closer to its pronunciation.

bay and amphitheatre which contains the city. For some time, we continued to follow the edge of the lake. The water had receded many years ago for some distance from the shore and so some of the extensive totora reeds beds had been replaced by some small fields of the local crops of corn, quinoa and barley. Beyond the reeds, the blue waters of the lake glistened in the morning sunlight.

Occasionally we would pass a small farm on the other side of the road. Its walls were made of adobe bricks as were its several enclosures. Rooves were often of thatched reeds or, in more prosperous farms, with earthenware tiles. As if to encourage the Englishman, many farms had walled-enclosures in which a few sheep were grazed. Gradually the road wound itself up into the low hills surrounding this part of the lake and so the view changed into a more austere landscape of dry, rocky slopes and the occasional adobe farmhouse and its fields separated by stone walls.

We passed through several small villages; Acora and Ilave, each with their adobe-walled houses and small open shop fronts. Several of the more important buildings were of two stories and were white-washed and painted in bright colours. The people on the dusty streets went about their daily tasks, carrying bundles upon their backs or shepherding small flocks of sheep out of the way of the coach. Sometimes the children would give a cherry smile and wave as the coach rattled passed. A well-made sign above an ornate arch leading into the village of Ilave had proudly announced that it was the capital of the Aymara Nation.

It was almost nightfall when the coach eventually pulled into the small coaching station next to a comfortable-looking posada on the edge of the town of Juli[7]. It had been white-washed and its timbers painted a bright green. Garcia and I were shown to our rooms and a good meal of local fish,

[7] Juli (pronounced "hooli") is nestled amongst several high, rounded and bare hills and is situated a little back from the lake.

corn and potatoes was prepared in the small dining room.

The Englishman and his wife sat at a separate table and generally poked at their food to show their mistrust of the local cuisine. Personally, I found the fish to be excellent. The Englishman leaned over in our direction.

"Well, a' least ya 'ave more types of potatas an' corn than we do at 'ome!" he said with a mouthful of food."

The Undertaker and the student ate quietly at their separate tables and did not venture into any conversation.

After the meal. Garcia and I decided to have a short stroll before taking to our beds. There was a narrow road leading downhill which was well lit with small lanterns and we assumed that it led towards the centre of the town.

The small canyon of adobe buildings with their red tiled rooves soon opened up into a broad plaza. It was well lit with lanterns and a few open braziers stood near several of the shops with the general appearance being one of cleanliness and order. The plaza was well planted with trees and shrubs, many of which had been cut into a variety of pleasant shapes. It was also pleasing to note that many of the buildings surrounding the plaza had been painted in a variety of pastel colours. The good people of Juli obviously had considerable pride in their town. I noticed however the lack of the usual prominent church building fronting the plaza.

An old man sat smoking with his dog on a stone bench opposite the small fountain which stood in the centre of the bushy plaza.

"Good evening, sir." I said, "this is a very beautiful plaza that you have here."

The old man slowly removed his pipe and looked up; a broad smile on his brown, lined face. "Thank you, sir, it is indeed a fine place for an evening smoke and a good evening to welcome strangers to our little town."

Garcia and I sat down on the bench next to the old man. His dog, also of a good age, got up and moved down to the end of the bench closer to its owner.

"I notice that there is no church in the plaza, although I can see what looks like a government building over there in the corner." I pointed to a small, but ornate building with an imposing entry archway.

"Ha! you are very observant, sir. Our churches are too grand for our little plaza, but we have many here just up one street or another!" he laughed. "Perhaps our little square once was much larger with churches all around and the shops and houses came later!"

He tapped his pipe onto the edge of the bench and put it back into his shirt pocket under his faded poncho.

"You know," he said, slowly waving his hand around as if to encompass his whole town. "Our little town is called the 'Rome of the Americas' because of our many churches."

He turned around and pointed towards a small opening near one side of the plaza. I could just see in the evening light that this led into another small garden and beyond stood a stone edifice almost completely hidden by the buildings fronting the plaza.

"Over there, you can just see the Cathedral Church of Saint Peter, the Martyr[8], so I guess that makes us a city, Yes?" He laughed. "It is also called the Church of St. Thomas Aquinas and it

[8] Iglesia Catedral de San Pedro Mártir

was started by the Dominicans in 1565 but the Jesuits had to come and finish it several years later. It was built in the Baroque style but you will see some of the influence of we Aymara people also in its construction with beautiful birds and other animals in some of the carvings.

You perhaps wonder that I, an old man, should know so much about our churches? Well, there you are. We are proud of our 'little Rome' and I also have the honour to be the Sacristan of our most famous church, the Church of Saint John Letran[9]. Come. I will show you its treasures."

With that, the old man got up, straightened his poncho and walked slowly off towards the other side of the plaza. His old dog followed with an equally sedate amble.

---

[9] Iglesia de San Juan de Letran – the name 'Letran' probably is derived from 'Laterin' – the name of several buildings in Roma, including the Lateran Palace, which stood on land once owned by the Lateranus Family of ancient Rome.

Garcia and I followed the old Sacristan past the garden of the old cathedral and up another narrow street sheltered by over-hanging buildings. After walking for two blocks, we stood in front of a small and rather plain church building. It was in the usual cruciform shape and built with packed earth. The bell towers seemed to be of Romanesque style and some of the dull brown covering was now starting to peel away in several places. My first impressions were not those of awe and wonder.

The old man stooped and produced a large, ornate key on an equally ornate chain from below his poncho. With some deliberation he carefully unlocked one of the doors and bade us enter. It was dark inside but he soon kindled a light from a nearby flint box and lit several candles standing in a large brass candle-stick holder near the door.

The effect was amazing and I did then stand in awe and wonder at the sight which I now beheld. The long nave was bare of all furniture but its walls were covered on either side by several large paintings in wide, ornate guilt frames.

"They depict the lives of the saints and especially the life and martyrdom of saint John the Baptist" said the old Sacristan, now drawn up to his full height and proud of this building in his care. "They date from 1570 it is said that they were painted by those who call themselves the 'Cuzco School'[10]."

I was greatly impressed by the paintings and the overall effect which they gave in the candle light. Their rich gold-leaf frames and the huge and ornate Altarpiece which was also richly encrusted with gold, sparkled in the gloom of the long nave and its roof of wooden arches.

[10] The Cuzco School or *Escuela Cuzqueña*, founded by the Italian Jesuit Democrito Bernardo Bitti (1548–1610) who came to Juli in the 1570's. Cusqueña paintings are characterized by their use of red, yellow and earth colours, their lavish use of gold leaf and their lack of perspective.

Garcia and I stood with the old man admiring the paintings for some time in wonder that such beauty could be found in a small, country church. But that is not unusual in this part of the world.

Eventually, Garcia and I said farewell to the old Sacristan and his old dog, dropped a few coins in the offering box at the door and walked back to the Plaza de Armas and then back to our Posada.

Novena Historia: La Virgen de Copacabana
(Ninth Story: The Virgin of Copacabana)

The next morning, after a very restful night in a comfortable bed, Garcia and I went downstairs for breakfast. It was a simple affair, as was usual in these parts; warm bread rolls with jam, fresh fruit and sweetened coffee. There was even the option of a fried egg which I declined.

The coach had already loaded our baggage and I noted that the passengers who had taken the seats up on top of coach now had changed but seem to be of similar type; traders with baskets of fruit and small hand-made goods going on to the next village.

There were the usual pleasantries as our fellow travellers inside the coach again resumed their seats. The Undertaker gave us a gruff 'good morning' and took the far window seat without any ceremony, much to the Englishman's disgust at having to wait his turn. His wife bustled into the cabin, finding her many skirts and hand luggage to be of some hinderance. Her husband attempted to assist by giving her a gentle push from behind before heavily climbing aboard with considerable expenditure of breath. Garcia and I followed and then the student nimbly took his seat with a shy smile as though he had been caught at missing lectures.

There is something about beginning a journey early in the morning; people are still recovering from the previous evening's revels or still in that level of consciousness which sleep has yet to relinquish.

Today, according to our coachman, we would be again travelling around the borders of the lake but now heading more to the east towards the border with Bolivia only fifty kilometres away. There would be a stop and change of horses at the border of course and then on to Copacabana. The coach would then go on to the lake crossing at San Pedro de Tiquina for the night before making the crossing of the narrow strait by punt the next day.

The countryside did not change that much although there seemed to be a few more trees, widely spaced, along the dusty road. They gave some comfort in the usual barren nature of the low hills and rocky outcrops which seem to be the usual landscape around this part of the lake. The small farmhouses of thatched adobe and the many fields separated by rock walls continued. People, both men and women trudged along the road; some carrying bundles on their backs or walking behind their small burros overladen with produce or firewood, a scarce commodity in these parts.

We passed through the small village of Yunguyo which was not far from the border. Its many small houses and shops were huddled close together in the bright thin air of the new day along the dusty road. Some of the shop owners were beginning to open the broad shutters to display their merchandise and some customers lounged against the walls waiting for other shops to open. The few dogs in the street also waited patiently.

Eventually the coach stopped next to a small shop which was open with its owner standing in the street beckoning us all to come into his shop for refreshment. The dusty travellers from the upper seats climbed down and opened their own earthenware flasks of water or chicha and small packages containing corn, potatoes, tamales and perhaps some dried meat.

It was too early for my own lunch, but Garcia, being of a practical nature, had brought with him a small package containing bread and some sangrecita[1] left over from breakfast. The Undertaker had remained outside and the student had purchased a small flask of local juice. The Englishman had taken my advice and had

---

[1] Sangrecita is a blood sausage made from chicken blood and seasoned with garlic, onion, chili pepper, herbs and often prepared with baked potatoes, fried sweet potatoes or cassava.

ordered two cups of mate de coca to assist with his adjustment to the thin air of this altitude as well as for his mid-morning refreshment. The tea was naturally served in rough, earthenware mugs rather than the chinaware that his wife had expected. She delicately tasted the beverage and pulled a face of disgust and handed the mug back to her husband.

"Perhaps the señora would prefer one of our excellent local fruit juices? "I suggested to her husband who now stood with two mugs of mate and a look of uncertainty on his face. He brightened up at my suggestion and I turned to the owner and said in Spanish:

"I am sorry, the mate is not to the señora's taste. Could she have some jugo[2] please?"

The owner soon returned with a glass of fresh juice which the 'good lady wife' tasted

[2] Jugo is fruit juice, often made from pulverising fresh fruit and is more like a Western 'smoothie'.

suspiciously at first and then drank with some relish. Her husband was most pleased and she also voiced a quite 'thank you' to me in appreciation.

To the horror of the Englishman, the coach then departed without its passengers. He stood open-mouthed and with his hand up pointing in a gesture of bewilderment after the receding coach.

"Do not worry, señor," I said "the coach is merely going on to the Bolivian customs office on the other side of the border. The coachman had completed all of his formalities with our customs officers here and we must do that also. You see? Our customs office is just across the road."

I pointed to the small white building across the dusty street where the sign over the arched doorway read 'Control Migratorio Peru'.

"After that, I am afraid we will have to walk up the hill and cross the border by foot. It is only a short way and after some more formalities we will again board our coach."

The Englishman and his wife had not expected to walk today and made the short journey up the hill with some difficulty. Garcia, being an honourable man had taken up the lady's small travelling bag with a gentle 'permítame, señora' and helped her and her husband up the road and under the broad, stone archway which was decorated with a faded sign which read 'Bienvenido a Bolivia[3]'.

The formalities with the Bolivian Custom's Officers were friendly and quickly over. Our travel documents, being complete had passed inspection without any enquiry. The Englishman and his wife were questioned briefly about their intensions in La Paz and I was able to act as translator so they too passed inspection.

---

[3] 'Welcome to Bolivia'

Our coach was parked outside and the horses where stamping their feet and nodding their heads ready to go. Everyone clambered aboard, pleased with themselves that there had been little delay at this border crossing and so we commenced our journey towards Copacabana. Just up the hill, a road marker indicated that it was just eleven kilometres away and soon the coach was rattling its way down the hill which led into the city.

My first impressions of Copacabana were very favourable. The city was nestled between several hills around a single broad bay; the waters of Lake Titicaca a sparkling blue in the midday sun. For the most part, the houses were of two or even three stories, painted in a variety of bright colours and most were roofed with dark red tiles. The streets were narrow as was typical of most towns in the Andes with people going about their business and dressed in a variety of mixed local and European garb. My almanac informed me that the good people of Copacabana were mostly of the Aymara people, as at Puno in Peru; the Spanish simply drawing a border through the lake to mark their own personal political territory with little regard to natural or local indigenous boundaries. It was the same all over this continent as peoples and often families became separated into different national populations.

Our coach stopped at a small yard within the city not far from the waterfront. This and its adjacent building acted as the coaching station. The passengers on top of the cab soon gathered up their bundles and quickly merged into the small crown which had gathered to meet the coach; some to greet the newcomers, others to await their turn to board the coach for its departure for the overnight stop at San Pablo de Taquina, further towards La Paz.

Our fellow travellers from the cab alighted and stood around adjusting their clothing or taking their baggage which was being handed down from the roof of the cabin by the assistant driver.

The Undertaker we noted with some interest took his small bag and quickly disappeared into the crowd. The student gave us a shy smile and faint wave of goodbye and went into the building to wait being called for the next leg of his journey. The Englishman, now occupied with his wife's fussy concerns and being in a new place surrounded by foreigners, looked over and gave us a nod of farewell and then they joined the student.

I had taken the trouble to telegraph ahead from Cuzco to book into the hotel which we hoped was the one indicated in our cryptic letter from Teniente Rivera and looked around for a representative from it. A little way from the coach stood a tired-looking old man dressed in drab European working clothes and standing next to a small pushcart. He was holding a small sign with the name 'Vázquez' chalked upon it. I had to quickly remind myself that this was the false name under which we were travelling. I quickly walked over to him and identified myself, motioning to Garcia to join me. We placed our small bags near the cart

The porter went to the elaborate ritual of loading our small luggage onboard his handcart and with a beckoning arm led us up a small, cobbled lane towards the large hill which dominated the eastern side of the city.

"That is the Cerro Calvario[4]," he said, pointing up to the top of the hill, "it is an important site for the pilgrimage. You have come for this perhaps, señores?" He asked, grunting under the strain of pushing his cart which only partially occupied by our meagre luggage.

"No, my friend, we are just simple travellers here on business. We have yet to explore your lovely city." I replied.

[4] Calvary Hill

With that he brightened up and stood more erect, now pleased that he now could be the tour guide rather than a lowly porter. He put down the handle of the pushcart and pointed up to the summit of the rocky crag which was above us.

"Why, señores, that is a most important place here in Copa. It is said that up there is the spot where, in 1697 a poor man with bad eyesight came across a mysterious llama which then spat into his eye as these animals often do when startled. From that moment he was able to see with extraordinary clarity. This miracle made his vision became so impressive that he was the envy of all the local people who then created a replica of the fourteen Stations of the Cross on top of that very hill."

Having told his story, our guide bent over and picked up the handles of his cart and continued his laborious journey up the cobbled lane.

Soon we came out onto a wide street which traversed the hill and on the corner with it and our lane stood an imposing three-story building made out of whitewashed stone and with several tall glass windows facing the road.

The words 'Posada Nueva España'' were proudly written in red on a yellow board which jutted out from the corner of the structure. The entrance way was of a double glass door which the porter pushed open and welcomed us inside.

Whilst this was clearly a colonial-era building, it was obvious that the old Spanish style had been greatly modified. The entrance archway with the usual double wooden doors had been replaced by attractive, modern double glass-panelled doors which opened into a narrow foyer with a side door which led into a well-lit dining room. On the other side of the foyer was an office and front desk. This foyer opened out into a wide, spacious area which would have been the interior courtyard of an older Spanish house. However, whilst it retained the surrounding upper galleries off which the rooms were entered, the courtyard was not completely open to the sky. There was a roof made of beams raising to a central point in its crown. There were many skylights around the edges of the roof made of framed yellow glass which gave the entire interior a cheerful, sunny glow. The central fountain was still there but the usual gardens had been replaced by many potted plants, mainly of the cacti variety and the rest of the floor was painted in dark green and covered here and there with rugs decorated in the Incan style. Several tapestries depicting local motives hung from the walls on the ground floor which, like their old Spanish counterparts contained few doors and no windows.

A jovial man with a broad smiling face emerged from behind the foyer's counter. "Greetings, señores! welcome to 'The Nueva España'. I am Señor Robles your host. Señor Vázquez, I presume?"

"Thank you, Señor Robles. This is my companion Señor Lorca." I said using the family name of Garcia's mother. "We should be staying here for a few days. I am sorry that I cannot be more specific but we are awaiting our friend who will also be staying here. Perhaps he has already arrived – he would be coming from La Paz?"

Señor Robles smiled and went back behind his counter and opened a large ledger which had been sitting on the top of the desk. He opened it and turned several pages.

"Ah! There is indeed a single booking coming from La Paz, a Señor Porteños and he is indeed expected soon. He telegraphed his booking from Buenos Aires about two weeks ago and should be here within the next few days, God and the roads willing." He laughed. "Meanwhile, let me take you to your rooms. Manuel will bring up your bags."

I confirmed with Señor Robles that his expected guest was indeed our friend and asked if we could be alerted when he arrived. I was rather put back by the choice of pseudonyms which our friend had used, as the term 'porteños' simply meant 'the people of the port', a common term which many people of central Buenos Aires used when referring to themselves. I hoped that this was not common knowledge here in Copacabana which was also a port albeit on a much smaller scale.

Walking into the spacious courtyard he swept his arm around and said with a smile of pride. "This is our grand foyer should you wish to rest. There is a table with fruit which we put out each day and a jar of coca leaves should you partake. There is always water boiling in our kitchen which the Night Manager would be happy to provide you with should you need mate de coca in the night."

I smiled at this courtesy often given to guests who have trouble with the altitude. "Thank you, Señor

Robles, but my friend and I come from Cuzco and are both suited to these heights, but we do enjoy mate de coca, never-the-less."

"A-ha!" he laughed, "then we will see you in our lovely dining room for mate de coca with our complimentary breakfast starting at six," he said, pointing through another double set of glass doors which opened into the grand foyer.

We thanked him for his courtesy and followed Manuel who was now walking up the stairs to our rooms on the second floor. He had indicated that the bathroom was just a few doors along at the corner of the landing as he opened the door to our room. Here we found our room to be simply but tastefully furnished with two comfortable beds and adequate hanging spaces for our clothing. An old-fashioned mahogany and marble-topped washstand with its large white porcelain pitcher and basin stood below a large mirror fixed to the wall. I gave Manuel a few extra coins for his hard work and introduction to his lovely city. He touched his forehead and gave us a huge grin.

"Many thanks, señores, I am to be found at the door behind the small desk in the far corner of the grand foyer should you ever require my humble services," he said and quietly closed the door as he left.

Having settled our things in our room, Garcia and I went downstairs and out onto the street. The posada had been built high up on the hill and so we had a commanding view of the city. The overall view was one of orderliness with many brightly-coloured buildings and several long streets running down from the rugged hills behind the city down to the sparkling waterfront on the lake. Here there were clusters of small boats and sever long jetties reaching out into the water. Over on the far side of the city was a large cathedral of imposing size and painted uniformly in white, with several copper domes and a tower of several spires.

We walked down the hill through the small cobbled lane up which we had come with Manuel. There was a storm developing across the lake which was known for its turbulence during such times. The sky had become very dark, save for a fiery red glow which shone like an angry eye just above the hills to the west. A sudden bright flash of lightning hit the water some ways off from the shore so Garcia and I hurried for shelter. We walked quickly down into the Calle Santivañez[5] where we found a small café. Having partaken of a good meal and some of the local wine, we returned to the posada for a good night's rest thankful that there would be no more coach travelling the next day.

The next day, being a Sunday, Garcia and I decided to go to Mass in the impressive cathedral that stood on one side of the city. At his desk, Señor Robles was in a talkative mood and, very proud of his city, told us that the beautiful

[5] Santivañez Street, named after the city in central Bolivia.

cathedral down the hill and across the plaza was called the Basilica of Our Lady of Copacabana and housed the statue of the Virgen de Copacabana, the patron saint of all Bolivia. He had also said that it had been constructed on the site of an earlier Augustine chapel, itself being built on the original temple sacred to the Incas. The Basilica itself began many years later in 1668 but was not completed until 1805.

It was a fine, sunny day and the lake sparkled in the early sunlight; Inti the sun smiled on Copacabana that morning.

Walking up to the Plaza, we passed many small street stalls. Here the ladies of Copacabana, many in their wide skirts, brightly coloured shawls and bowler hats sold a variety of produce. These included a vast array of nuts, fruit, sweets, small jugs of chicha and flower petals of many colours. I was intrigued by the latter two commodities for I had noticed that several of the cobbled streets leading up to the plaza had been decorated in various religious motives formed by sprinkling the flower petals on the cobbled street.

As we walked up Calle La Paz, approaching the plaza, the decorations increased in number and complexity; the colours becoming more vivid and the shapes within the decorations more intricate. There were many stalls now near the plaza and I asked an elderly lady sitting next to her stall what was the occasion for such decorations.

"Why, señor" she replied, "it is usual on a Sunday for the priests to bless the animals and carriages of the people. Later in the day after Mass, the priest will come and bless all of the animals and the carts of their owners, even the handcarts!" she laughed.

"Thank you, Mother." I replied "but what are the purposes of the small jugs of chicha? Surely it is not for the priests?"

The old lady's deep brown lined face was split with a huge grin.

"Oh no, señor! the priests or the owners take the chicha and after the priest has sprinkled holy water onto their cart, the owners will pour a little chicha onto their carts or animals so that some of it will fall to the ground. It is to honour Pachamama[6] and so give some extra meaning to the blessing. Of course, what the owners and the priests do with it afterwards is their own affair," she said with a chuckle.

I thanked the old lady who no doubt thought that we were uncouth strangers not to be aware of such local customs. We walked across the neat plaza which is planted with many shade trees and has a beautiful statue of a young woman at its

[6] Pachamama is the old Incan goddess of the Earth and fertility. The rite of pouring some of one's drink onto the ground is called *challa* and in many places of the high Andes it is considered good manners to do so when offered a drink. Pachamama is often equated with the Virgin Mary in many rituals.

centre. In front of the imposing white basilica with its coloured and patterned domes and brown edging, was a long line of several more stalls, all decked with garlands of many colours and a great variety of other trinkets. Garcia and I decided that we would visit these after Mass. Up the few steps we walked into the forecourt of the basilica, passing a rather grand statue of some robed personage near the main entry. Inside, we were struck by the beauty but relative simplicity of the interior, save for the rich alter and a small niche containing a richly-decorated stature of the Virgin. The walls of the main nave were painted white and the supporting columns were yellow. The vaulted domed ceilings were pale blue with a spider-web of arches in orange. The overall effect was most pleasing.

The Mass was given in the usual way and by an old priest who gave a spirited sermon on the virtues of gaining strength from the Scriptures. At the end of the Mass, Garcia and I waited until most of the faithful had left and I approached the priest who was standing at the entry door farewelling his flock.

"Excuse me, Padre," I said as we came up to the old man "could you please tell me who is the person carved in such a beautiful statue?" and I pointed to the statue which stood just outside of the entryway.

The old priest looked up and then around to see who else was coming out of the nave. Then he looked into my eyes and smiled.

"You are strangers here, I can tell. Why, this is our famous carver, Don Francisco Tito Yupanqui who carved our magnificent stature of our Blessed Virgin of Copacabana who you would have seen inside. She is the patroness of all of Bolivia!"

I was startled by the name of the sculptor for this was also my mother's name. The old priest noticed my surprise and quietly asked:

"Is there something wrong, my son?"

"No, Padre, this man bears the same name as my mother's people. She was Doña Valentina Ruiz Yupanqui and it would be a rare coincidence for her to be related to this man."

The old priest again looked around and seeing that we were alone, motioned us over to the base of the statue and sat down on the narrow plinth.

"That is indeed an interesting coincidence. What was your mothers' ancestry? "he asked.

I sat down next to the priest and Garcia stood a little way off admiring the activities at the stalls in the plaza. I introduced myself and Garcia using our false travelling names and told him about how my mother could trace her ancestry back to the Capac Incans, the highest rank of the nobility of the ancient Incan peoples of Cuzco.

The old priest, who had introduced himself as Father Sancho, looked at me and then up at the face of the statue.

"An interesting coincidence, indeed Don Hernán. Would you care to hear the story of Don Francisco and the Virgin of Copacabana? I have a little time before my brothers and I must go and bless the animals and their carts."

I was now very excited. My mother never spoke very much about her ancestors, it was always my father's people who took pride of place. Perhaps it was some mark of shame or perhaps protection that the Spanish side of our family always came to the fore in conversations.

Father Sancho looked up again at the statue and then out towards the plaza and told the story of Francisco Tito Yupanqui, the carver of the statue of the patroness of Bolivia.

"It was around 1580 when the harvest had been very bad and there had been other calamities as well so the people had become frightened and wanted some divine help. Despite having received the Christian faith, they were still attached to their original religion but never-the-less some decided to erect a statue and dedicate it to the Virgen de la Candelaria[7]. Unfortunately, the various factions in the town could not decide upon this dedication and so nothing was done." He said, his arms going up in a gesture of hopelessness.

"That is the way of many town committees' I replied in consolation.

---

[7] More correctly *Nuestra Señora de la Candelaria* – Our Lady of the Candles or simply the Virgin of the Candles. She is named from a statue which was found by two goatherds in the Canary Islands in 1392 and she holds the Christ Child in one arm and a green candle in the other. The veneration of the Virgin Mary, through this statue was carried over to South America with the arrival of Spaniards who came from the Canary Islands.

"However!", Father Sancho continued, "one man, Francisco Tito Yupanqui, who was born in Copacabana but was a descendant of the Inca, Huayna Capac[8] did not abandon the idea and conceived the project of carving an image of the Virgin who would help the people. This amateur sculptor, helped by his brother Felipe, worked the image of the Virgin in clay to represent all of the natural graces of Mary. But alas, they were but poor fishermen and so the image was not very good and it was placed on one side of the altar by Father Antonio, the parish priest at that time. However, when Father Antonio left the Parish, his successor ordered the poor image to be removed from the church. Francisco Tito, humiliated by this setback, went to Potosí well to our south where he found an outstanding master of sacred images called Diego Ortiz who taught him how to sculp in wood. With this knowledge he decided to again work on the final image of the Virgin de la Candelaria. Finally, after much opposition from

---

[8] Huayna Capac, (Quechua: "the young mighty one" - 1468–1524) was raised in Cuzco and was the eleventh emperor of the Inca civilization.

some of the other factions, the statue was finally brought to Copacabana on the second of February, 1583. You see!" said Father Sancho pointing out into the plaza, "we have even named our lovely little plaza to honour the day that the Virgin came to our city - the Plaza 2 de Febrero[9]. Our Virgin is made of dark mahogany wood, so she is often known romantically as Morena, the Dark Virgin or the Black Madonna."

Father Sancho folded his arms and sat contented, having told his story which explained many questions which had entered my head since arriving in Copacabana.

"Thank you, Padre", I said "have there been any miracles attributed to the Virgin – after all, she is the patroness of your country?"

The old priest looked up with a little sadness in his eyes that such things should be doubted.

[9] Plaza of the Second of February.

"Many, My son. Perhaps the most famous one occurred many years later when two men from Brazil visited the city. Not knowing the capricious nature of our lake, they went fishing way out upon its deep waters. You saw yesterday perhaps, how quickly a storm may come up. Yes?"

"Yes, Padre" I replied, "the darkness and lightning were most violent."

"It is true!" continued Father Sancho, "these poor fishermen feared for their lives and prayed that they would be saved. It is said that they saw a vision of the Virgin of Copacabana who guided them safely back to shore. In gratitude, they had a replica of our stature made and took it back to their home country where it was placed into a small chapel near the beach at the city of Rio de Janeiro. Here the chapel received many devotees and so they renamed the barrio in honour of the Virgin of Copacabana."

Décima Historia: El Legado del Comandante
(Tenth Story: The Legacy of the Comandante)

It was several days later that Señor Robles, the manager of the posada, stopped us as we were going out for our usual morning walk down to the waterfront.

"Excuse me, señores! your friend, Señor Porteños arrived late last night on the coach from La Paz. He is in Room 21 should you wish to visit him later; the coach was very late, you understand."

I thanked him for his understanding and decided to let our friend have a few extra hours to sleep. Garcia gave a quiet chuckle and we left the posada and walked down the Calle Jáuregui[1] to the small bluff which overlooks the lake.

We caught up with our old friend and former goaler at a late breakfast. When he saw us enter

[1] Palace Street – often from surnames derived from the Basque word for 'palace' or 'manor house'.

the dining room, he jumped up for joy and embraced us both. "It is good to see you again Colonel!" he stammered.

I held my finger up to my lips to alert him to the use of my rank and motioned to him to sit down at his table. We joined him and quickly ordered breakfast.

"Well, now, Señor Porteños!" I said, placing some emphasis on his assumed name, "I am so glad that someone from the port was able to make it so far inland!" I jested. "Permit me to name my friend Pablo Lorca" I said placing my hand on a grinning Garcia's shoulder," and of course, you remember me, your good friend Doctor Hernán Vázquez."

The young man gave a conspiratorial smile at the use of our names and replied: "mucho gusto[2], señores! I have a lot to tell you…"

---

[2] "Nice to meet you!" – a standard greeting in Spanish.

I interrupted him again by putting my finger to my lips. There were only a few guests of the posada still at breakfast, but I thought it expedient that we discussed our business in a more secure place.

We finished breakfast and I led the way out of the posada and though the streets to the Plaza 2 de Febrero. Here we found a quiet seat in one corner of the plaza where some trees shaded us from the early morning sun. It was still too early for the old men to come to the plaza to play chess or discuss the woes of this Earth, nor for los lustrabotas[3] to bother us with their trade.

"It has been a long time!" I began, "what is it now, five or six years since you were our gaoler at San Rafael?" I laughed.

[3] Los lustrabotas, or *lustras*, are the shoeshine boys and a familiar sight in many plazas. Around La Paz, the biggest city of Bolivia, they are often masked so that friends or relatives do not see them in this lowly trade and the term *lustrabotas* is a derogatory one; the correct, dignified name is *lustracalzados or lustra calzados — 'one who uses shoe polish'*

Gabriel looked first at Garcia and then at me with downcast eyes for we had sat down with him in the middle.

"Yes, it has been some time Colonel…sorry, Don Hernán. Many things have happened. I am a Capitán now and attached to the Legal Service of the Headquarters of our army. After we left San Rafael, I returned to Quito and completed the final year of my Degree in Law whilst staying in the army attached to our Headquarters. When I completed the degree, they gave me a promotion and appointed me to the Advocate General's Office.

"A fitting position for the man who assisted in our execution!" Garcia and I both laughed at my gibe. We remembered back to when Garcia and I, on an exploring mission for the Peruvian Army, had been captured by the Ecuadorians in the jungles which had become disputed territory and taken to the fortified hacienda of San Rafael at Baños de Agua Santa in the mountains of

Ecuador. Here we had been treated as honoured guests by the old soldier Comandante Antonio Castillo Andrés and all of the happy family at this supply depot, including its young Second-in-Command, Teniente[4] Gabriel Rivera Peña who now sat between us. In time, our presence had become a political embarrassment to the ruling junta[5] as our countries were not technically at war, so they decided to simply get rid of the evidence. They had sent a representative, a 'fixer', out to oversee our executions. Don Antonio, however had conspired with his lieutenant to fake our execution. He had also enlisted the services of another good friend, Brother Dominic, San Rafael's padre to provide me with the 'last rites'. It had been a very tense situation, as the three of them had not confided in any of our other friends at the hacienda least one would inadvertently give the plot away. I was not aware of my salvation until Teniente Rivera had tied the

[4] Lieutenant.
[5] Junta (pronounced 'hoonta') - a military or political group that rules a country after taking power by force.

blindfold around my head and told me to flinch when the bullets passed by and act as though I had been killed. Nor had his Firing Squad been told of the change in circumstances until he had walked along the line of men exhorting them in a loud voice, for the benefit of our unwanted guest from Quito, to shoot true; and then in a quiet whisper to miss me entirely but aim as close as possible. I had no need of faking my shock as the bullets hit the wall a few centimetres from my body, for the Lieutenant had already chosen his best shots for the firing squad. Garcia had also suffered accordingly; he had been taken out by another group of men to be executed away from the hacienda. The trustworthy Sargento Pérez had been given his secret instructions just as Garcia had been loaded onto a wagon with our three wounded men whom had been brought from the town's hospital. The doctor, another friend of the Comandante would, of course, provide the Junta with the appropriate Death Certificates. Our 'burials' had been a great success and our little party of fake corpses had been loaded up onto a wagon, along with some very tasty supplies, and taken south along the lowland road to friends who would see us safely across the border. It had been a trying time, but the memory of our faked executions had also rekindled many thoughts of kindness to our friends at San Rafael.

"And have you heard from our old friend the Comandante?" I asked.

Gabriel looked down at the ground and slowly said in a low voice "the Comandante died a few weeks ago, I am sorry."

Garcia and I sat for a while, remembering the kindness of the old soldier and father to all at San Rafael.

"I am sorry too, Gabriel. He was a most honourable man. There are few like him left in this world."

Garcia made the sign of the cross and said something in his native Quechua which I did not pick up; a short prayer perhaps.

"I will tell you how it came about," said the young Captain, now looking older than his years.

"Please go on" I said and he told us the story of the Comandante and San Rafael.

"I received a letter from the Comandante's daughter earlier this year. You will recall perhaps that at the time of your execution, it was the Junta's plan to close San Rafael and erase all knowledge of what had happened at San Rafael. They had sent a large sum of gold to ensure the Comandante's silence along with an honourable retirement from the army and instructions to return all of the supplies held in the depot and close down San Rafael. Of course, being a good man, he took the gold and had his friend Brother Dominic spread all of it around his needy flock. Our soldiers were also discharged or transferred to places near their homes, although many of our local men simply disserted and returned to their farms taking whatever they could from the old hacienda; with the Comandante's approval, of course. I was given a transfer back to Quito with the recommendation that the army assist me in my legal studies and make the appropriate appointment to the Legal Service following my graduation.

Everyone was happy with the arrangements: the man sent from the Junta, a dishonourable and an ingratiating individual, Capitán Carrasco Flores went back to Quito with the good news of a well-ordered execution; the Comandante retired with honour to his daughter's home in Colombia; our garrison troops were able to go to their homes with some degree of wealth; and you and Garcia could return to your own homes in Peru. No one knew of the whole story. But back to my story.

I said that I had received a letter from the Comandante's daughter, Doña Antonia saying simply that her father was ill and that he wished me to come at my earliest convenience. On the face of it, it would seem a rather simple letter about the health of an old friend. Unfortunately, to me it meant much more. The phrase 'at my earliest convenience' was one that the Comandante used professionally when an army unit requested more supplies as a matter of great urgency involving a life-threatening situation. It was our own private code which we used with our outlying units. A sort of joke making fun of the Supply Branch's tardiness in supplying anything immediately when requested. I knew then that the Comandante wanted to see me about some matter of life and death and that he wanted me urgently.

As it would happen, I had also received a telegraph from my Aunt in Buenos Aires that my uncle, my late father's brother, had recently died. I used this family tragedy to visit the Comandante for his use of our code also suggested some secrecy.

I then set about requesting compassionate leave to visit my Aunt and made arrangements to travel to Argentina through Colombia; it being a quicker route to go via the Caribbean Sea and down the Atlantic coast to Buenos Aires. All of these arrangements I made through Headquarters and so when I headed north on the earliest coach to Colombia, everyone in our Headquarters knew of my intensions and all of the appropriate travel papers had been arranged.

Once I had crossed the border heading north to Cartagena on the Caribbean Sea, I secretly made arrangements with the coach driver to get off at Pasto and headed west on another coach to Tumaco where I was met by Doña Antonia's people and taken to her estancia[6]. Later I would continue my journey to Cartagena and take ship around the coast to Buenos Aires. From there I would continue on up the length of Argentina and then into Bolivia.

[6] Estancia – a large ranch used for cattle or sheep.

Arriving at Doña Antonia's estancia, I was saddened to find that Don Antonio was on his death bed and was not expected to live much more than a few days. A Jesuit priest, had come up from Quito to hear his confession and give him the Last Rites and...."

"Let me ask" I interjected "was this Jesuit called Father Xavier?"

"Why yes!" Gabriel replied somewhat startled, "do you know him?"

"Garcia and I had the pleasure of his company on the coach from Puno. He seems a remarkable man but I am thinking that he may have been more than the Comandante's confessor." I ventured.

The young man sat for a while in silence. A gentle breeze through the trees in the plaza seem to make the silence even more pensive.

"Perhaps you are right Don Hernán, for I have seen Father Xavier several times at Headquarters in Quito, but I thought nothing of it at the time."

"It may be that whatever secret the Comandante wished to impart may has also fallen on other ears. We will have to keep on our guard. But what was it that was so important that the Comandante wished to tell you on his death bed?" I asked.

"That is it, Don Hernán! it is still a secret!" he said looking puzzled. "I was able to see him alone for a few minutes whilst he still had some strength. He gave me two letters; one which I was to post to you when I reached a safe city, which I did at Buenos Aires, and the other a sealed letter which he implored me to hand it over personally here at Copacabana. He also said that the fate of both our countries may be at stake and that it would mean a return to San Rafael."

"Ah! and I had already deduced that it was you who had sent the letter from Buenos Aires. But it was the Comandante who knew about your story of the little gaucho and that we would come because it was your request!"

"That is so, Don Hernán. I was simply told to take the sealed letter to Copacabana by July the twenty-third…which is in three days, so I have made good time."

With that, he loosened his cravat and reached down inside his shirt front and pulled out a cloth wallet which he had on a small cord around his neck. Opening the wallet, he brought out a thin, brown envelop which he handed to me.

It was a non-descript envelop, the kind common in many military Orderly Rooms, and I carefully broke its seal and drew out the document inside. The paper was of the finest quality and the writing was in a hand which I had seen often whilst a prisoner at San Rafael; that of Comandante Antonio Castillo Andrés. In his hand, now of weaken strength it read:

My Dear Colonel Moreno,

By now you have met with my good friend, the young Capitan at Copacabana, a pleasant city which I had visited in my youth and one far from the intrigues of both Quito and Lima.

I was certain that you and Garcia could not resist another adventure and our countries need your help. The young Capitan has gained sufficient knowledge to assist in this quest but needs the cunning and physical support that only you and the formidable Garcia can provide.

Unfortunately, you will need to take the long journey and return to San Rafael to solve the final puzzle of this quest. I am sorry that I could not be more specific but I could not risk this letter and the secret of San Rafael falling into the wrong hands. Once you have found out this secret, the next course of action will be apparent to the young Capitan and then he can assist in solving the crisis which will soon befall both our countries. By the time this is over and you all have returned to Quito, the young Capitan will find another letter at his office containing a list of influential men who will help with this salvation. This list will be disguised as a list of 'Persons of Suspicion Requiring Military Investigation' but this will be far from the truth, for these good men can be trusted beyond question and are well-placed in the highest circles.

To uncover the secret of San Rafael, you will need to go to where we spent many an evening over Amontillado and my fine cigars. May the force of Jesus help you in this quest. It is written in the scriptures that:

'Forasmuch as ye are manifestly declared to be the epistle of Christ ministered by us, written not with ink, but with the Spirit of the living God; not in tables of stone, but in fleshy tables of the heart.'

May God bless you all,

Antonio Castilla Andrés.

Undécima Historia: La Ciudad Blanca
(Eleventh Story: The White City)

And so, it was that we resolved to return to San Rafael in the mountains of Ecuador near the town of Baños de Agua Santa. There would be only three possible ways of completing our journey; one which may be fraught with danger as our destination may be known to others.

That evening, Garcia, Gabriel and I sat around one of the tables in the open foyer of the posada, a large map of South America in front of us. As there were no other guests in the foyer, we had decided that this was as safe a place as any. Our choices of route seemed to amount to only three: Return the way that Gabriel had come with a long and arduous journey down the length of Argentina and then an even long sea voyage followed by more travelling across Colombia; to return to Puno and then travel by coach back to Cuzco and then up the length of Peru into Ecuador, coming along the Amazonia road to get to Baños by the east; or to return to Puno and travel down the mountains to Arequipa and then on to Matarani and take a ship to Guayaquil the sea port of Quito in Ecuador and then by coach into the mountains to Baños. Whilst the first route was very long and would take many weeks, it was secure. The second route would be along roads well-known to us and there would be friends to help if needed but it also would also take considerable time and have many arduous couch journeys. It was decided then to take the third alternative and return to Puno and take the train to the Peruvian coast and then a steamer to Guayaquil in Ecuador. Such a route would be faster and more comfortable and there would be less chance of interference by others.

Garcia has some reservations about our proposed route as he had neither travelled by train nor been down to the sea; he was a true Andino and rarely left his beloved mountains.

The next morning after breakfast, we packed our bags, paid our account and said farewell to Señor Robles and his comfortable posada. There was a coach going to Puno within the hour so we walked down to the corner to the coaching office and purchased our tickets using our assumed names and occupations; I was again to be Doctor Vázquez the academic travelling with my secretary, Pablo; and Gabriel would travel as Señor Porteños, a lawyer. He would be travelling under the guise of going to Guayaquil to undertake some legal transactions and would appear to have made our acquaintance only at the posada. I had telegraphed ahead to my hotel in Puno for our accommodation and had also enquired about the railway services to Arequipa and further on to the coast. We were in luck on this point, as our couch would arrive in Puno the next day and a train left for Arequipa the morning after. We would again have an overnight coach stop at Juli and our papers were in order for crossing the border back into Peru. Our return to San Rafael was starting in good order.

The coach trip to Puno was uneventful; we shared the cabin with a young government official and his family and there was the usual small group of local people and their bundles occupying the seats on top of the coach. We did not venture out after arriving in Juli but stayed in the inn and enjoyed some small reminiscences over a few glasses of excellent wine. Arriving in Puno later the next day, we again walked the short distance to our posada on the Avenida La Torre. It was pleasing to note as we passed the rather plain building, that the railway station was at the end of that avenue only a short distance from our posada.

It was also only two blocks away from the small plaza which fronted the Jesuit Church of Saint John the Baptist and I was interested to enquire after Father Xavier who had said that he had business there. So, the three of us walked down Calle Oquendo which narrowed down to a small lane and led out into the small plaza and to the church. My friends decided to wait on a seat in the plaza with our few bags whilst I went up the steps to the entrance of the church. It was not Sunday, but as was the custom, the gates and doors to the church were open. I took off my hat and entered. The nave of the church is very attractive with yellow painted walls and a plain white ceiling. Around the alter, the walls are painted shades of blue representing the sky with faint clouds. Skylights on either side of the roof above let in light which greatly enhances the natural effect of the surrounding walls. High up in the aqua-coloured altarpiece is a richly gilt niche containing the Virgin of the Candles, the patroness of Puno.

An elderly man, dressed in a plain dark robe was placing flowers in the vases set on two brass stands. "Good, morning, sir!" I said quietly, and he turned and with a gentle smile replied.

"And also to you, my son. I am Father Ignatius. May I help you?"

"Thank you, Padre I was hoping to find Father Xavier with whom I travelled down from Cuzco a few days ago. Is he here?"

"Alas no, my son, you have missed him by a few days. He was only here briefly to bring me some documents and then he left."

"Do you happen to know where he went to from here, Padre?"

"Back to Cuzco, I assumed my son. He had been working there for a time I believe. I am sorry."

I thanked the old priest who gave me a silent blessing before I left and I gave a few coins to the old lady sitting on the steps near the entrance.

Walking down to my friends in the plaza, I said "the mysterious Father Xavier has moved on; perhaps back to Cuzco or elsewhere. I feel that we may run into him again, so keep on your guard."

We continued our walk to our posada on Avenida La Torre and settled in for the night. Early next morning at breakfast, Garcia the reliable soldier was excited. "When does the train leave Patron?"

"Do not worry, Garcia. We have plenty of time." I replied.

An hour later as we checked out of the posada, Garcia looked at the clock in the office and asked me the same question again. He was like a small boy going on his first holiday.

With plenty of time to spare, we left the posada and walked down to the station. Here we found the usual crowd of people waiting to board the train which sat patiently at the single platform, its engine panting and sighing like some impatient beast ready to slip its leash. Garcia ran up the platform and stood next to the engine. He had never seen a steam locomotive before and to him this was a great wonder. To him the locomotive did seem to be alive and he examined all of its exterior as though he was appraising a new mule or donkey. The Engineer gave him a friendly wave and the Fireman shovelled more coal into the firebox. The fantasy had been broken.

Garcia returned to where Gabriel and I were standing. I had been able to buy three First-Class tickets to Arequipa and again reminded Garcia and Gabriel to assume their aliases before boarding. Garcia took out the plain glass spectacles and straightened his best set of clothing to once more assume the guise of the dutiful servant and scribe. Gabriel had no problem with his disguise as 'Señor Porteños, Lawyer' as he indeed looked the part in his austere black suit, although I suggested that he did not offer his name here as the station was situated in the Barrio Porteño[1].

Garcia paced up and down and asked me again for the departure time of the train in fear that we

[1] The suburb of the people of the port – situated on the edge of Lake Titicaca.

might miss it. Eventually the Station Master ordered that the doors be open and the people formed up in their queues to enter: the Third-Class passengers lifted up their bundles and waited stoically for their turn to board and take their hard bench seats; the Second-Class passengers also formed an inpatient crowd at the end doors to their carriages; and those who held First-Class tickets stood back and waited patiently to enter. Our carriage, like the rails and locomotive, were of American manufacture and consisted of a central aisle with rows of padded seats on either side in groups with some facing forward and other facing back. The timber work was partly ornate and dirty glass flagons of water with a pair of glasses hung from their fitting above each window. The groups of chairs were separated by a low barrier above which were ornate brass luggage racks. This would be a lot more comfortable than our dusty coaches and there would be an opportunity to get up and stretch one's legs should the need arise as it would be a good eight hours before we reached our destination.

Garcia sat next to the window facing the direction of travel and I sat next to him. Gabriel took the other window seat opposite Garcia and I was pleased to find that the other seats in our group would probably be unoccupied as the carriage was only partly filled as the train started its journey with a sudden jerk of the carriages and a sound of its steam whistle. Garcia looked apprehensive.

Rail journeys are always a fascination for me. One can watch the landscape passing by in relative comfort. Despite the rattling noises, the carriages bouncing on the track and the occasional whiff of cinders coming through the open window, rail travel is much more enjoyable than the cramped confines of a shaking carriage on narrow dusty roads. Garcia enjoyed this entertainment and was pleased that he could get up and walk around the carriage. He found it also pleasant that he could go to the small outside balcony at the end of the carriage and have a cigar. He soon found several like-minded souls who would join him in conversation and he could once more be simply Pablo Garcia from Cuzco again.

Our train started northwards around the lake and eventually came to the city of Juliaca where it carefully made its way through the streets and part of the local market. This was an interesting passage, as normally the street would have given itself over completely to the stall holders and individuals with small piles of vegetables or handicraft. Almost every item conceivable was on display for sale or trade: there were the usual tables of fruit and vegetables; covered stalls with pieces of meat and a variety of fowls; wooden handicrafts; earthenware containers of a variety of shapes and sizes; small pens of donkeys and llamas; and even large collections of metal parts and components. All of this would be moved ever so slightly to allow the passage of the train through its crowded midst. I felt that this was somewhat analogous to a modern, urban parting of the waters the passengers hanging out of the windows watching this spectacle were the lost tribes of Israel being led by a puffing black mechanical Moses.

Having carefully negotiated the market without losing even one item on offering, the train briefly stopped at the rather plain-looking station of Juliaca where some passengers alighted and others came on board. I noted that most who got off were from the Third-Class carriages and carried bundles, no doubt destined for the market through which we had just come.

Now our train turned and took the western line that would take us down the slopes of the Andes to Arequipa, almost three hundred kilometres to the west and over fifteen hundred metres lower down in altitude. For the most part, the countryside was flat and it was only much later as we entered the river valleys which ran down the slopes to the sea, that we noticed that our journey had always been downhill. The view generally was one of extensive open plains, treeless and covered in either small stones, with a backdrop of bare hills and sometimes the cone or ragged slopes of a snow-covered volcano.

After several hours in which the arid landscape had become monotonous, the train came to a slow, creaking stop at Imata to refill the locomotive's water tank. Imata was a small village in the middle of an expanse of rocky desert with its distant line of arid hills and one central ribbon of light brown, dusty compacted earth represented the highway joining Arequipa to Juliaca. Behind the few poor houses which opened onto the road, the long stretch of lonely rail vanished into the distance.

Whilst the Engineer saw to the refilling of the water tanks, a few passengers got off to stretch their legs on a surface which was at rest if not a lot dustier. Local people with a variety of foods and other wares wandered along the side of the carriages encouraging the occupants to purchase their goods. There was considerable activity at the Third-Class carriages where the inhabitants had waited for this chance to restock their food and drink supplies. Some trinkets and a few food items were sold to those of the other carriages. The local baker had learnt from considerable experience that his tasty empanadas[2] were a popular item at all classes of carriage and he soon turned away with an empty basket and a full pocket.

It was late afternoon when our train pulled slowly into the station at Arequipa, having bravely negotiated one of the most hostile of landscapes. Even though there had been some opportunities to sleep; the gentle swaying and jingle of the carriages tended to induce such rest, we all stood

[2] Empanadas are crescent-shaped, savory pastries popular in many South American countries, especially Peru. They are made of dough and filled with a variety of ingredients such as beef, chicken, pork, tuna, shellfish, cheese, olives and / or vegetables, seasoned vibrantly, then baked or fried to perfection. Delicious!

with some degree of muscular stiffness and a general feeling of lethargy. We took our small bags down off the racks above our heads and slowly and carefully clambered down the small steps which led off the end balcony onto the stable firmness of the platform.

Outside the glass doors of the Waiting Room were a large number of small, brightly painted carts all advertising one hotel or posada or another. The owners yelling loudly at encouraging the tired passengers from the First- and Second-Class carriages to accept their offers of transportation to their establishments. The Third-Class passengers generally ignored such entreaties and shouldered their bundles and shuffled their way through the barricade of carts and donkeys and dispersed into the waiting crowd beyond.

I led the others over to a blue cart labelled 'Posada Yanahuara' in striking yellow letters and signalled to the driver that he now had three clients for his establishment. Garcia noticed the name and turned to me with some recognition in his eyes. "Yanahuara!" he exclaimed "The tribe who wore black shorts!"

Gabriel looked at Garcia and then at me to find some meaning in Garcia's excitement.

"Yanahuara, indeed, Garcia, for that is the meaning of their name," I replied, throwing my bag onto the back of the cart and climbing up to one of the seats. "You have remembered the story which I once told you when we were guests at San Rafael."

Gabriel and Garcia had likewise thrown up their bags and settled themselves on the seats which ran the length of the cart down both sides. I turned to Gabriel.

"Yanahuara is a well-known part of this city. It refers to the people who once lived there who were always identified by the black shorts common to their tribe. Once when Garcia and I were taking our leisure at San Rafael one morning, I told him the story which I had heard when I was here very many years ago. It was about the Simpleton of Yanahuara[3], a poor but brave man who died protecting a lovely lady from the brutality of her husband. Perhaps I will tell you of it tonight after dinner."

The Posada Yanahuara proved to be an excellent choice even if I did choose it out of sentimentality. Like many of the buildings on Calle Beaterio to the west of the city, it had been constructed as a private home in the early 18th Century and made out of the white, volcanic stone which the locals call *sillar*. Many of the grand buildings and older private homes of the centre of the city are made out of this hard, waterproof and beautiful volcanic rock, giving the city its title of The White City. This is indeed appropriate, for Arequipa is a beautiful place and one which I had come to love

---

[3] See '*El octava carta - el simplón de Yanahuara*' ('The eighth letter – the simpleton of Yanahuara'), in the book LETTERS FROM SAN RAFAEL (Felix Publishing 2018)

on my first trip as a young soldier those many years ago. I had been told in jest then, by an old man whose people had been here before the Spanish conquest that the name really referred to the place where Los Blancos - the whites – lived referring to the Spaniards who founded the city in 1540 as 'Villa de la Asunción de Nuestra Señora del Valle Hermoso de Arequipa[4]'

Our posada had the usual inner and outer courtyards with balconies around both and rooms on the upper floor for guests with the ground floor rooms for the owner's family, guest lounge and kitchen. The rooms were airy and well-furnished and the service provided by Señor Suárez was most comforting after our long journey.

[4] 'Villa of the Assumption of Our Lady of the Beautiful Valley of Arequipa' – the name Arequipa probably comes from the local Quechua language *"Ari qhipay"* meaning *"Yes, stay"* when confronted by the Spaniards.

Having settled our things into our room, we decided to walk into the city and find an agreeable restaurant for the evening meal. Señor Suárez had recommended 'La libertad', a restaurant upstairs near the steps of the Cathedral. It was a balmy evening for that time of year as we walked together happily down Calle Beaterio and onto the bridge which crosses the Chilli River which cuts through the centre of the city.

Midway, I stopped and pointed to the east where the majestic and perfect volcanic cone of the volcano El Misti stood with its snow-covered top standing out like gold illuminated by the final rays of the setting sun.

"Look there!" I exclaimed, "that is the Volcán El Misti – 'The Gentleman'. See how it sits like its name suggests between two other volcanoes – Chachani to the left and Picchu Picchu, the smaller one on the right."

"Ah!" said Garcia who was happy to hear his native Quechua replied "those names mean 'The Beloved' and 'Top Top' "

"Indeed, Garcia." I said, being also fluent in that language, "they look peaceful now in the late afternoon sun, but this city has been subjected to eruptions and earthquakes in the past. Let us hope that they do not decide to wake up tonight!" I laughed.

Gabriel had turned his attention to the Chilli River flowing with some force and turbulence under the stone bridge. The waters, like most rivers on this side of the Andes flowed through the desert only because of the snow on the nearby peaks such as El Misti.

"Don't worry, Gabriel. This is the Francisco Bolognesi Bridge. It was named after our great hero of the War of the Pacific who defended the town of Arica from an overwhelming force of Chileans and who would not surrender and said when asked to surrender that he would fight *"hasta quemar el último cartucho[5]"* – the famous motto of our army. This bridge has been here since 1608 and I doubt that it will fail now just because the Chilli is showing some anger."

The young lawyer looked over the parapet of the bridge at the swirling white and brown river below.

"Oh, but I must warn you, Gabriel!" I continued. "You must never go down to the river's edge whilst it is so angry. They say that the waters are also inhabited by sirenas[6] who will entice you into their realm if you are not careful, especially if you are pining for a love that is lost."

Gabriel looked up and laughed; that of a man who is uncertain about the truth of the matter.

---

[5] "Until the last cartridge has been fired"
[6] Sirenas are mermaids or river sirens.

We continued our walk across the bridge and up the street lined with archways containing shops which sold a variety of goods, from food to tapestries and musical instruments. Soon we came into the large and beautiful Plaza de Armes of Arequipa. It was a most remarkable, almost festive scene. Far across the well-tended gardens with their tall palms was the impressive broad façade of the Cathedral Basilica of Arequipa. It seemed to have been built in a classical, Romanesque style with many columns built into the wall of carefully cut white sillar stone. Small lamps at the base of each of these columns gave the front of the cathedral a friendly glow. There were tall lampposts spread throughout the plaza which was surrounded on its other three sides by white, two-story buildings fronted by many arch colonnades. The building opposite the cathedral contained government offices upstairs but all of the other buildings contained many small shops behind each arch and cafes and open spaces above. We walked across the lovely plaza which was crowded with people out enjoying the night.

Our restaurant was upstairs in a building in the north-eastern corner of the plaza with its tables set out on the arched balcony overlooking the very steps of the cathedral where several hawkers plied their trade selling small watercolours and religious trinkets to the passers-by.

The next morning, after a generous breakfast of warm rolls, pastries and spreads with fruit juice and coffee, we packed our bags, said farewell to our host and walked again across the bridge and then south the few blocks to the railway station. Here we found our carriages in the same position which we had left them the previous afternoon. Apparently, the rail authorities thought it prudent only to travel the short distance of a little over one hundred kilometres to Matarani on the coast in daylight hours. At the appropriate boarding time, we took our seats in our First-Class carriage and continued our journey.

Initially we travelled through the same arid countryside of bare hills and occasional small, rocky plains. Then the track seemed to twist and turn as it negotiated some of the stepper sections which led down onto the narrow coastal plain which was also a desert. There was little to be seen in the way of vegetation and even the town of Matarani seemed to have been built up of the same earth as the dusty brown desert which surround it. Only a few green tops peeking over high adobe walls suggested that some houses at lease had some greenery. There did not seem much of interest as we walked to the nearest hotel from the station.

Matarani was a small port town which was now becoming very important because of its shipping which was mostly concerned with the export of mining and woollen products from the mountains and Arequipa. Luckily our ship was already in port and due to sail that evening, so we made went directly to the shipping agent to book our passage.

The ship was the *S.S. Mariana,* an aging steamer which still retained two masts rigged for sail. The clerk at the agency of the East Pacific Steam Navigation Company proudly informed us that the *Mariana* had been built in Scotland in 1872 and was of iron construction and of 852 tons displacement and, most important the clerk stressed, she was British registered and would take about four days to reach Guayaquil in Ecuador given favourable weather.

She was essentially a cargo vessel but would also take a few passengers such as ourselves. She plied the route between Valparaíso in Chile and Panama City stopping at Matarani and Callao in Peru and Guayaquil in Ecuador. Her cargo was anything which was available, but Matarani was the main port for the interior woollen trade but mining equipment and some mine products were also shipped. The clerk was very adamant that she did not carry any of the nitrates from Chile; a somewhat explosive cargo!

It was early evening before we were allowed to board and were greeted at the top of the gangway by a white-coated steward of Asian appearance who took us several decks below and along a very narrow companionway to our cabin. It was a four-berth cabin consisting of two sets of double bunks with tubular steel rails on either side of the upper bunks and a tall wooden vanity unit below the small porthole situated between the bunks. The steward quickly showed us how the wash basin was lowered down by pulling down the door of the vanity unit and explained that he would fill the water tank above and remove the waste tank below every morning. There was a small mirror inside the vanity unit above the wash basin which was served by a single tap. Our other toilet needs were served by four chamber pots under the lower bunks. There were no wardrobes as passengers were expected to bring their own travelling trunks for the purpose of holding their clothing. There were, however several coat hooks on the walls or 'bulkheads' he called them, which would hold our clothing.

There was a small mat on the wooden floor between the bunks and a single electric light at the end of each of the upper bunks. In parting, the steward announced that there was also a communal bathroom at the end of the companionway and that dinner would be served in the Saloon sharply at six - and that a good standard of dress would be expected. His last comment was made whilst looking in the superior manner that only stewards and butlers could achieve, at Garcia and his dusty clothes.

We made out arrangements in the tiny cabin with some bustling and Garcia took one of the upper bunks so that he could see out of the small porthole. He was used to the open spaces of the Altiplano and such a confining space unsettled him greatly. He had also been astounded at the breadth of the sea when we arrived in Matarani. Lake Titicaca had been the biggest expanse of water that he had ever encountered and it worried him greatly that he could not see any mountains or other land on the wide blue horizon. Gabriel took the other upper bunk as I mistrusted such elevated beds and preferred one of the lower bunks. Our bags were stacked below the lower bunks and this allowed the other lower bunk to be used for personal items when dressing.

Having made ourselves as presentable as possible, we went up on deck and made enquiries as to the location of the Saloon. It was aft or at the rear of the ship and down one deck. Entering, it was a different world to the untidiness of a cargo ship's deck with its variety of machinery, masts, coils of wire rope and myriad rust stains along the deck and down the ship's side. Here we found a comfortable and spacious cabin; wood panelled with brass lamps and fittings and a well-set, long wooden table.

We were greeted at the door by the captain himself; Captain Ridgeway, a solid character with a full beard, now greying at its edges, and a smiling tanned face which gave testimony to his many years at sea.

"Welcome to the *Mariana*!" he said in an open jovial manner, "she's not much to look at, but a sturdier ship you'll not find on this side of the Americas. Señores Vázquez, Porteños and Lorca, I presume. Welcome aboard. Please, find yourselves seats at my table. We have few formalities here – we are not an ocean liner you know" he laughed. "I'll be with you shortly. We have some more guests arriving."

We thanked the captain and sat down along one side of the long, highly polished oaken table which fill most of the rear section of the cabin. Three other men in faded blue uniforms sat on either side at the end of the table and were obviously the other ship's officers. They stood up as we found our seats and gave us a collective brief nod and smile. The tableware was up to the standard of an ocean liner and I suspected that

Captain Ridgeway had once had pretensions of commanding such a vessel.

Soon the other guests arrive. These consisted of only one couple who appeared to be a European merchant and his wife. The lady gave us a brief smile as they sat down and the captain took his seat at the end of the table. Our white-coated steward entered, was given some quite instruction by the captain and then left.

"It is our informal custom at our first meeting for each of us to give a brief self-introduction and so I will start with myself." The captain stood up, gave a short bow and introduced himself as 'Captain Joshua Ridgeway, Master of the *Mariana* and English by birth'." These gentlemen here "he said motioning to his officers. "are my officers; Mister McLaren my Engineer is from Scotland as seems to be traditional on many of our ships..." he said with a quiet laugh "... my First Mate Mister Riley from Belfast and my Second Officer Mister Rodríguez is Peruvian from Arica, which was once in Peru but by the misfortunes of war is now part of Chile. My Third Officer, Mister Connor cannot be with us at present as he is overseeing our departure. He is an American and I am sure that you will meet him soon but you will probably hear him well before you do." he laughed. "I must also give you my apologies in advance as I will have to leave somewhat early to take the ship out.

Upon hearing their name, each man had stood and gave a short nod of his head as he was introduced. The captain sat down and looked at me as I was sitting closer to his end of the table. I stood up and gave a brief smile to all those around the table: "Permit me to introduce myself and my colleagues. I am Doctor Hernán Vázquez, an academic from Cuzco and this gentleman to my right is my secretary, Señor Pablo Lorca. My other companion sitting next to him is Señor Gabriel Porteños who is a lawyer and we are from Peru." I felt that a minimal identification was in order for the time being.

The merchant stood up in his turn and introduced himself as 'Mister and Misses Henry Entwistle from Leeds, England' and he was a 'financier'. He did not seem a person of sparkling personality and I imagined that such an important position as 'financier' would not allow for much humour. Misses Entwistle, however was all smiles and obviously proud of her husband and his lofty position.

The steward came in again and handed a small menu card to each of us.

"This is Filipe, our steward." Captain Ridgeway said, waving a calloused had towards the steward who responded with a toothless grin. "Please feel free to make any of your needs known to him. He will be nearby this saloon for most of the day and there is a small electric bell button at the end of your companionway should you require his services at night. Now to our dinner menu."

The small card contained the contents of our forthcoming meal. It was printed in rather ornate script and the small food stains down its length suggested that it had been regularly used. It read:

Soup of the Day: Julienne
Fish: Boiled Rock Fish with Butter Sauce
Meats: Haricot of Mutton or Bœuf au Four
Vegetables: Potatoes baked or boiled; Mashed
Turnips; Green Beans
Deserts: Rice Pudding or Apple Tart
Cheese Platter: selected local cheeses and biscuits.

Garcia looked at the menu trying to decipher its contents as he had no English whatsoever. I quietly gave him a quick translation in Spanish but that did not improve his appetite for this English food.

"I would recommend the mutton, tonight, ladies and gentlemen" said the captain which suggested that perhaps the beef was not up to standard or even aboard. My suspicions were reinforced over the next few days as mutton seemed to figure most prominently on the menu disguised as such British delicacies as 'Irish Stew', 'Shepherd's Pie' and even an 'Indian Lamb Curry'. No doubt the captain was a great lover of lamb and the couple from Leeds, England seemed to enjoy their meals.

Gabriel and I had been exposed to a variety of European foods, but Garcia obvious missed his Andino fare and so was very selective in his choices at meals but he did find that he had a distinct liking for rice pudding.

Just a little before seven, Captain Ridgeway stood up, wiped his beard with his napkin and took his leave. Soon the vibrations coming from below decks became more pronounced as the S.S. *Mariana* headed out to sea.

Duodécima Historia: El Caballero de Los Mares
(Twelfth Story: The Gentleman of the Seas)

Our voyage was a pleasant one as the seas for a change along this rugged coastline of Peru were calm for the most part. Captain Ridgeway in one of his rare moments of meeting him on our short promenade deck, informed us that with the wind behind us and the Humboldt Current[1] running freely, we would be in Guayaquil by Tuesday morning.

That evening at dinner, Captain Ridgeway, as was his nightly custom, called upon his youngest officer, Mister Connor, the American, to give a toast to the British king, Edward the Seventh whose portrait took pride of place on the bulkhead behind the head of the table. It was

---

[1] The Humboldt or Peru Current is a cold, low-salinity ocean current that flows north along the western coast of South America and is named after the Prussian naturalist Alexander von Humboldt (1769 – 1859). The deserts of Peru and Chile are due to the current and prevailing winds which flow north and off shore rather than blow water eastward onto the land.

strange for us, being trained in the armies of our countries to make this toast without standing, but the good captain had explained that it was the custom of the Royal Navy to make such toasts in the sitting position since the days that King William the Fourth had cracked his head on the deckhead[2] when serving with the Royal Navy over one hundred years ago.

It being Sunday, Mister Connor also gave the Toast for the Day which was 'to absent friends'. It seemed strange to us also that an American should be giving the toasts appropriate to the British Royal Navy, but Captain Ridgeway gave a simple justification for his custom by saying that this was a British ship and that he himself had been in the Royal Navy or 'the Andrew' as he called it, in his youth.

---

[2] Deckhead is the ceiling of any ship's cabin as opposed to bulkhead which are the walls. In early sailing ships, the deckhead was often much less than the height of a standing person.

Dinner on Sunday nights also seemed to be one of the Captain's traditions and consisted of a lamb roast with all the usual English trimmings of baked vegetables, green beans, Yorkshire pudding, gravy and mint sauce. At least there was an excellent Argentinian Malbec[3] to complement the food.

After dinner, Captain Ridgeway stood up, the deckhead being just a short distance above his head, and announced that it was also the custom for an after-dinner speech to be given by one of the officers. Tonight, it was the turn of the Second Officer Mister Rodríguez. Applause and the captain sat down.

Mister Rodríguez, to use his formal maritime rank rather than his Spanish honourific of 'señor', stood up and pulled a small sheet of paper from his tunic. He was a tall, thin man with the

---

[3] Malbec is a red wine. The grapes are known as one of the six grapes used in the blend of red Bordeaux wine. It is also celebrated as an Argentine variety of grape.

complexion of a southern European, that is with pale brown skin, brown eyes and black hair which glistened with a light application of hair tonic. He had thin, black pencil moustaches and I could not help thinking that he would be more at home in the salons of Lima than from the small coastal village of Arica, now part of Chile. He seemed quite young for the position of Second Officer; I guessed that he would be not more than in his late twenties.

He cleared his throat and looked around the table with his dark, penetrating eyes.

"Señora y señores…" he said, lapsing into his native tongue "…forgive me. Ladies and gentlemen, it is my honour to give the Sunday speech" he continued in good English.

I would have to give some brief translations to Garcia and Gabriel who had little understanding of that language.

"As we are still in Peruvian waters, I would like to talk about one of our great heroes of the most recent War of the Pacific. I do this as a Peruvian and in deference to our three guests here tonight who are also from my country. May I ask if any of you gentlemen speak the English?" he looked rather earnest with this question and he seemed now more like an undergraduate student giving his fist dissertation rather than a lothario from Lima.

I gave a brief nod of my head." Thank you, Señor Rodríguez." I said in my best English, "I would be delighted to give a brief progressive translation, please continue."

"Muchas gracias, Doctor Vázquez" he replied with a small bow. "I will now tell you the story of Almirante Miguel Grau Seminario, Peru's most famous sailor; the man that both the Peruvian and Chilean Navies called 'el Caballero de los Mares' or in English, 'the Gentleman of the Seas'."

The young officer lowered his eyes which were now wet with tears. "I had the honour to be a very young Alférez de Fragata or as you would say Second Lieutenant." He looked over at the captain, "I do not think that we have a rank of Midshipman but anyway, I had the lowest rank of officer in the navy and it was my first posting, you understand."

The young officer then consulted his notes but I think that his story came more from his heart than from his sheet of paper. He went on and gave his story about the Gentleman of the Seas.

"Almirante Miguel Grau was born in the coastal town of Paita, which we will be passing tomorrow, in 1834. He entered the Paita Nautical School and first went to sea when he was nine years old, aboard a merchant schooner and later in other sailing vessels as he sailed all over the world. In 1853, at the age of 19, he left the merchant marine and became an officer in the

Peruvian Navy. His career was brilliant and promotion was rapid."

The young man consulted his notes as he continued. "In 1868, he was named commander of the *Huáscar*[4] with the rank of Lieutenant Commander and was later promoted to Commander. By 1874, he had become the commanding officer of all of the Peruvian Navy's fleet with the rank of Captain.

The *Huáscar* was our navy's flagship and was an ironclad turret vessel, that is, it was built of iron and had its main armament in a revolving turret on the deck. It was also equipped with a most formable ram in its bow. Some in other navies would call it a turret ram. It was built in Britain by John Laird Sons & Company and launched at Birkenhead in Cheshire in 1865. It was named after one of our rulers of the sixteenth century, the

[4] Huáscar (1503–1532) was the Inca who succeeded his father, Huayna Capac and ruled the Incan Empire from 1527 to 1532.

Inca Huáscar. I have some details of her construction if you are interested?"

Without waiting for a reply, he pulled another card from his tunic pocket and continued his talk. "She was described as being of 1,100 tons displacement, with steam engines of 1500-horse power driving a screw propellor which gave a speed of about 12 knots. She is 190 feet[5] in length, 35 feet in breadth, and 19 feet 9 inches in depth. She carried two Armstrong breech-loading 10-inch guns in one turret, several smaller canons on deck and a Gatling gun."

I was able to give a quick translation to my companions with some vague estimation of the conversion of the British units of measurement into our metric measurements. Garcia made a gentle sigh of approval when I mentioned the calibre of the guns. Second Officer Rodríguez continued his story:

[5] There are approximately 3.3 feet in one metre with 12 inches to the foot.

"When the War of the Pacific began on 5th April 1879, between Chile and Peru which had come to the aid of Bolivia whose coastal territory had been invaded, Miguel Grau was aboard the *Huáscar*, as its captain. In an impressive display of naval mastery, Capitán Grau then played an important role interrupting Chilean lines of communication and supply, damaging, capturing or destroying several enemy vessels, and bombarding port installations. The *Huáscar* soon became famed for striking by surprise; these actions initially prevented a Chilean invasion by sea. For his actions, Capitán Grau was promoted to the rank of Contralmirante, that is the equivalent to Rear Admiral in the British Navy. Very soon, on the 21st of May, the *Huáscar* came out of a thick sea fog and encountered the Chilean wooden steam corvette, the *Esmeralda*, captained by Arturo Prat Chacón, and two other vessels; the schooner the *Covadonga* and the transport *La Mar* in the bay at Iquique. This town was once in Peru and was being blockaded by the Chilean ships. It is now part of Chile and about two hundred nautical miles[6] south of Matarani."

Second Officer Rodríguez looked over at Gabriel with a look of enthusiasm and said, "You, Señor Porteños might be interested to know that the Chilean, Capitán Arturo Prat was also a lawyer! He studied whilst he was a naval officer and was accepted as a lawyer in 1876. He wanted to be a naval lawyer and made several reforms to the Chilean Navy's legal codes but regrettably he died before he could complete his work."

Gabriel blushed slightly as he had followed a similar course in the army of Ecuador and had finally succeeded in reaching the goal as a military lawyer. The Second Officer continued his story: "Now, the *Huáscar* came upon the Chilean ships quite unexpectedly and the two smaller vessels turned and fled further into the bay leaving the *Esmeralda* alone to fight the *Huáscar*.

[6] One nautical mile is about 1.8 kilometres.

This poor ship was doomed from the start: she was wooden against the *Huáscar's* armoured iron plate; she was smaller with smaller calibre cannon; and she could only travel at eight knots as opposed to the *Huáscar's* twelve.

Now the *Huáscar* had been accompanied by the Peruvian ironclad the *Independencia* captained by Juan Guillermo More who was ordered by Almirante Grau to pursue and sink the other fleeing Chilean ships. At a critical moment however, the helmsman of *Independencia* was shot by a sharpshooter aboard the Chilean ship *Covadonga* and, out of control, the *Independencia* ran aground.

Meanwhile, Capitán Prat had manoeuvred the *Esmeralda* so that it was near the coast but Grau moved in and began firing with her big guns at six hundred metres. The Chileans returned fire but their smaller shells simply bounced off the *Huáscar's* armour plate. To add to Capitán Prat's worries, the Peruvians on the shore had set up field artillery on the beach and a fortuitous shot had hit the *Esmeralda,* causing one of her boilers to explode. More shells from the *Huáscar* hit the unfortunate wooden vessel killing several of its crew. Now only able to steam at two knots, Prat manoeuvred his ship so than it was between the *Huáscar* and the Peruvian shore batteries. Unable to effectively use his cannons and wanting to prevent anymore slaughter, Grau ordered his ship to ram the *Esmeralda* which it did so at full speed.

It was said that on the impact between the two ships, the brave Capitán Prat jumped aboard the *Huáscar* with the cry of 'follow me, boys!' he was followed by Petty Officer Juan de Dios Aldea. But the two men found that they were alone as the noise of battle prevented the rest of the crew of the *Esmeralda* hearing Capitán Prat's words. Prat was immediately shot to death on the deck near the turret by one of the sharpshooters on the *Huáscar* and the gallant Petty Officer was severely wounded.

Grau gave orders for the *Huáscar* to stand off and allow the remainder of the crew of the *Esmeralda* to surrender. They did not, and fought on under the command of the ship's only surviving officer, Lieutenant Luis Uribe Orrego who had the Chilean flag nailed to the mizzen[7] mast.

The *Esmeralda* was rammed again but this time Sub-lieutenant Ignacio Serrano boarded *Huáscar* with eleven more men, armed with machetes and rifles but the Gatling gun of the *Huáscar* cut them down leaving only Sublieutenant Serrano the only survivor, with several shot wounds in the groin. Grau gave orders that he should be carried below to the infirmary and treated alongside Petty Officer Aldea. Not long afterwards, after being battered for over four hours the gallant *Esmeralda* sank below the waters of Iquique Bay, the Chilean flag still nailed to the mizzen mast flying until the waves broke over it.

[7] The rear mast of a ship

Almirante Grau, distressed at the plight of the very few survivors of the *Esmeralda* now fighting for their lives amidst the turmoil where their ship had gone down; ordered the boats of the *Huáscar* to be lowered to take the survivors aboard to be given all medical aid and comfort. They were our enemies but now just drowning men who must be saved from the sea. Out of a compliment of over two hundred men, only fifty-seven were rescued. Having secured all of the men and bodies which we could, our ship headed for our companion, the luckless *Independencia* which was aground. We took off her crew and then set her alight so that she would not fall into enemy hands.

After the battle and the lifting of the blockade of the town of Iquique, Almirante Grau sent Prat's personal effects such as his diary, uniform and sword among other items, to his widow. He also attached a personal letter describing the heroism of her husband and his own personal sadness in seeing the death of such a gallant officer, offering any assistance which was able to give. Grau also had the bodies of the dead Chilean sailors buried with full military honours on the shore of the bay. Because of his actions in the battle and later for his noble gestures toward Prat's widow and the surviving crew members, Grau became honoured in both Peru and Chile as a gallant naval hero and was now known by all as the "Gentleman of the Seas"."

There was applause around the table as the Second Officer sat down. Captain Ridgeway stood up: "Thank you, Mister Rodríguez for your most stirring personal account of the Battle of Iquique." He looked around the table and asked if any of us had any comments.

Henry Entwistle from Leeds, England beamed across the table and said: "What a grand event that battle must have been! Your story, Mister Rodríguez reminded me of the tales my father used to tell me when I was a boy. He sailed with Nelson; don't you know? Thank you for your account, sir."

The Second Officer looked over at our party sitting opposite with some anticipation of receiving some comment from his fellow countrymen, so I stood up.

"Señor Rodríguez, on behalf of my companions, may I congratulate you on your most exciting and gratifying story of one of Peru's greatest sailors, Almirante Grau Seminario, el Caballero de los Mares. Of course, even in the Altiplano we heard of his gallant exploits but not as well told as we heard tonight. Thank you. But tell me, since you were aboard her, what was the true fate of the *Huáscar*? The popular press only ever provides details of the victories in warfare, very rarely the defeats. We know, of course that she was eventually captured but for our curiosity and for the edification of Señor Entwistle, perhaps you could enlighten us on that event?"

The Second Officer looked at his captain who smiled and gave a brief nod of his head. Rodríguez again stood up but looked sad, again his dark brown eyes had a watery gaze. "Muchas gracias, Doctor Hernán Vázquez. That was a very heroic tale and a sad one. Regrettably I cannot give you a first-hand account of the end of the *Huáscar* as I was on shore at the time. I was the Signal Officer during the Battle of Iquique and spent most of my time in the armoured casement of the bridge with the Almirante. Unfortunately, when taking a message to the gunnery officer in the turret, our communications tube having been shot away, I received a slight wound and was taken to the infirmary. After the battle, the Almirante insisted that I be taken ashore with the rest of the wounded and given all the best care. He even wrote to my mother. The ship then sailed without me! Luckily I was evacuated from the hospital at Iquique and taken north before the Chileans overran the town in November."

The Second Officer hung his head and waited for a short time until his sadness passed, then he continued. "I will keep this story very brief, if you do not mind. My ship, the *Huáscar* sailed south to continue to harass the Chilean supply ships; she even captured a transport full of a regiment of cavalry. However, the Chileans eventually could not tolerate her interference any longer and sent a small fleet out to rid themselves of this lone raider. A few months later, in October of 1879, off Punta Angamos, which is about forty nautical miles north of Antofagasta, the *Huáscar* accompanied by the corvette *Unión*, encountered the Chilean fleet. This was under the command of Commodore Galvarino Riveros who had with him six ships including two armoured steam frigates, the flagship *Blanco Encalada* and the *Almirante Cochrane* captained by Commander Juan Jose Latorre. These two ships engaged the *Huáscar* whilst the speedier *Unión* was able to fight her way through the cordon and sail north to Arica.

Right from the outset, the heavier guns of the Chilean frigates caused considerable damage to the poor *Huáscar*. A shot from the *Cochrane* pierced *Huáscar's* turret, wounding the twelve crew members manning the 300-pound cannons.

Another shot perforated the armour just above the waterline, cutting the rudder chain leaving *Huáscar* temporarily adrift. Soon after, an armour-piercing shell from *Cochrane* struck the bridge casement, killing Almirante Grau, but the *Huáscar* fought on.

With the Almirante, her Captain and many of her crew killed or wounded, Lieutenant Pedro Garezon, now in command decided to scuttle the ship. Seeing the bad state of the ship, the Chileans closed in and boarded the *Huáscar*. The remains of Almirante Grau were buried in Chile with full military honours. In recognition of her gallantry, the *Huáscar* was taken into the Chilean Navy where she still serves as a reminder of her gallant crew." The Second Officer sat down and for a while there was silence.

Captain Ridgeway stood up, coughed and said. "Madam Entwistle, gentlemen, perhaps we should all adjourn to the rear of the saloon where I notice that Filipe has set out our coffee."

We stood up and made our way from the dining table. It was only then that I noticed that our tall Second Officer walked proudly, but with a distinct limp.

Decimotercera Historia: Una Reunión Inesperada
Thirteenth Story: An Unexpected Reunion

Captain Ridgeway's prediction about our voyage proved to be correct; both the Southeast Trade Winds and the Peru Current had ensured that we had a speedy passage to Guayaquil, the main seaport of Ecuador. The *Mariana* had taken on a pilot at sunrise before it steamed up the Rio Guayas and docked at the long Malecón[1] Simón Bolívar.

I awoke and asked Garcia what he could see out of the small porthole between the bunk beds as the ship had stopped and there was no longer any motion of the sea.

"We are at the dock, Patrón," he replied, reverting to his old habit of calling me Boss now that we were not in public view. "There is a long line of

[1] Malecón, el – Spanish term for a quay or waterside.

nice white buildings across a wide road next to the dock and we are next to some sort of crane for unloading our cargo."

After the usual English breakfast of bacon, sausages, eggs, and tomatoes, cold toast and insipid tea, I was looking forward to Ecuadorian fare which I hoped would be more to our palette. We packed our few belongings into our bags and said farewell to Captain Ridgeway who was standing at the gangway to see his few passengers off before attending to the more difficult task of unloading the rest of his cargo. The Entwistle's from Leeds, England, were not early risers so were still in their cabin. As we got to the gangway, I saw the thin Second Officer standing some ways down the deck. He looked sad that his ship had returned to land and gave us a slight wave.

"Have you been to Guayaquil before, Gabriel?" I asked my young companion as we walked down the gangway.

"Yes, Don Hernán. A few times. I came here first with my father when we had left Argentina and then later as a young officer. You must know that Guayaquil is a maritime city for the importing and exporting of goods. It has all of the usual bad places along the waterfront for the sailors. Most travellers go on to Quito or into the country but I believe that this city is still a good one with many beautiful parks and fine buildings. However, I was told that I should avoid the south side of the city at night."

Out onto the dock and the small park between it and the wide road which ran the entire length of Malecón Simón Bolívar, we found a small gathering of men with pushcarts and donkey traps waiting to assail any luckless passengers disembarking to offer them the patronage of their respective hotels. One man of gaunt appearance pushed his way through his fellow carriers to come up to where we were standing.

"Señores, permit me please to offer you the services of the Hotel Bella Vista; good rates, clean rooms and you can come and go at your earliest convenience...." He hesitated for a while and added "If you understand?"

Gabriel looked at me at the mention of the phrase often used by the Comandante at San Rafael for anything requiring some urgency – 'at your early convenience'. Perhaps it was just a coincidence or perhaps another one of the Comandante's legacies. I took the chance and motioned to the others to put their bags up onto the back of the small donkey trap. The driver introduced himself as simply Raul before flicking the reins.

Heading down the wide street near the docks, Raul did not make conversation but kept to the business of driving his small donkey trap through the narrow streets of the old part of the city. A quick look to the sun told me that we were heading south.

We turned into a broad street which had a long central strip extending down its centre. A sign post on a passing building announced our thoroughfare as the 'Avenida del Veinticinco de Julio[2]'. Soon we turned off the main avenue and headed east along a street called Calle los Esteros. It was a wide street with a variety of two-storey houses and shops on either side which suggested an area of modest habitation. A few hundred metres down the street we turned into a small arched alleyway which had a sign above it reading Hotel Bella Vista and below in smaller print Barrio de Justicia y Libertad. The façade of the building on the street was a plain one painted a light blue, with several windows faced by twisted, ornate bars. There seemed nothing of the beautiful view promised by the name of the hotel to be seen anywhere in the street and I hoped that this truly was a place of Justice and Liberty.

[2] Avenue of the Twenty Fifth of July – the date that the city was founded in 1538.

Thanking Raul for his service with a few coins and receiving a smile and a nod of his head, we took our small bags and went through the main door and into the foyer. Here we met a tall man of solid statue with just a mere hint of a smile on his strong face. He was an elderly man who stood straight and held himself with some pride. A former military man, perhaps.

"Welcome to the Bella Vista, señores. Permit me to introduce myself as Ramón Franco, the owner of this grand establishment and your host. If I can at any time you need assistance I will come at your early convenience."

The same phase used in the Comandante's old code. Perhaps now this was not just a coincidence. We would need to have our wits around us here in Guayaquil.

Raul returned to take our bags under his arms and lead us upstairs to a spacious room overlooking the street. There were four beds and several wardrobes, a table and four chairs and a wash basin and jug. He mentioned that the bathroom was at the end of the hall but added in a low voice that we would be safe here. Whatever he meant by that was indeed another puzzle.

The day had passed slowly; mainly in our room or walking in the large courtyard of the hotel. We had purchased some food and other items from a local shop and were sitting around our table discussing our future travel plans over a map of Ecuador which Señor Franco had given us. According to the map, we were only about 185 kilometres from Baños de Agua Santa and San Rafael – no more than about two or three days away by coach. But this was the problem; there were few coaches going northeast into the mountains and such public transport as was available, would naturally attract some attention.

There was a knock on the door. It was the owner Señor Franco. He came into the room and closed the door behind us. He had a worried look on his face.

"Señores, a note was given to me at the desk just a few moments ago by a lady. She was a very beautiful lady," he said with some concern.

I took the note, unfolded it and noticed that it had been printed in simple block letters which read:

'TO LEARN THE SECRET OF SAN RAFAEL COME TO THE PARK NEAR THE CHURCH OF SAN EDUARDO TONIGHT AT 10'

I looked up at the hotel manager: "A beautiful lady, you say?"

"Yes Señor Vázquez, a very beautiful lady. Not too young yet not too old, if you understand. Flashing dark eyes and long black hair."

The old man hesitated for a moment, then said: "Permit me to be plainspoken, señores, but I feel that this may be a trap!"

"You have read the contents, then?" I said looking up sharply.

"Well…I am sorry, señor. It seems to be the lot of people like me to read such messages, but I mean you well."

I relaxed a little and looked at my comrades then turned back to Señor Franco: "No matter. Yes, perhaps you mean well and I am sure that this message does not bode well for us. A trap? Perhaps! Thank you, Señor Franco."

Franco stood for a while not knowing what to say next. Instead, he gave a slight bow and withdrew, closing the door quietly behind him.

"Well then!" I said looking at my companions around the table, our presence in Guayaquil and our quest appears to be known!"

"We must take care, Patron." Garcia said in a tone which I had heard many a time before entering into a dangerous venture; usually in some out-of-the-way mountain pass or upon entering a jungle path.

"Yes, Garcia, we will! But I am curious to see what this note will bring, trap or no trap. Tonight, you and I will make this rendezvous but by our usual practice. You remember?"

"Yes, mi Colonel!" Garcia replied with the wolfish grin he often had when a new and dangerous situation presented itself. "We will go early and from a different direction than what would be expected."

"Exactly Garcia, I am glad that retirement has not dulled your wits. That is exactly what we will do."

"And what is it that you wish me to do, Don Hernán" Gabriel asked earnestly.

"Garcia and I are used to such subterfuge …although we have never carried out our explorations in a big city. Of course, we are well armed and should be able to handle a possible ambush, but you will be needed here to alert the authorities if we do not return by midnight."

"But…." the young man exclaimed.

"No Gabriel, you are needed here. You are a Capitán in this county's service and a lawyer to boot, so the authorities will listen to you and act swiftly if needed."

"It is because I am an officer in the Ecuadorian army that I should go with you. Yes, a Legal Officer to be sure, but I received the same combat training as any other officer," he replied.

"I am sorry Gabriel, but you must stay here. Your role is very important and we may need you. Now let us see where the Church of San Eduardo is located," I said, turning over the map of

Ecuador which the hotel manager had given us to reveal a street map of the city.

"Here we are on the Calle Esteros…. about here" I said, placing my finger on the approximate position of our hotel. "Ah! and here is the Iglesia Católica San Eduardo. It is quite close to us; southeast further towards the river, about…." I quickly measured the distance along the streets using the edge of the note…." just about little over a kilometre. The map shows a small park near the church's mission."

Garcia looked at the map and the location of our rendezvous, "our guests would expect us to walk openly down Calle Cotacachi coming from this hotel. But see here!" he pointed to the map just north of our objective, "there are a number of small alleys running off this Avenida 10A which connects to Avenida 10B on which the park is located. We could take this alley and come up to the park from the north rather than the west as expected."

"That is a good idea, Garcia, look here, Gabriel!" I looked up at the young man and pointed to the map. "Here is the church of Saint Edward and here is the park. At nine tonight, Garcia and I will walk down this alleyway and approach the park from the north. We will wait here and see who arrives. If we have but one host then I will approach and Garcia can stay in hiding. If there are several, we will withdraw and return here. Either way, if we do not return by midnight then you must bring help. Understood?"

"Yes, Colonel." Gabriel reluctantly agreed.

Having made our plans, Garcia and I checked our weapons. He had his knives and I had my revolver. There should be no problem. All we had to do now was to wait until nightfall.

Dinner at the Bella Vista was plain but well-prepared, it consisted of soup followed by a chicken dish. Señor Franco served us himself and looked worried.

"You are going out tonight, señores?" he said to no one in particular.

"Yes, Ramón" I replied, using his Christian name to show that he was now trusted, "and I will go out at nine to the park mentioned in the note with Señor Lorca, but Señor Porteños will remain here. Should we not return by midnight, he will contact the authorities with your help. If that is agreeable to you?"

"Yes, Señor Vázquez, as you will, but I feel bad about this meeting…..I have some men who can be trusted in a fight if you would want to take them with you?"

"Thank you, Ramón, but it should be alright. Señor Lorca and I have been in many bad situations together," I confided.

Promptly at eight that evening, Garcia and I once again checked our weapons and put a little food from the kitchen in our pockets. Garcia had found a small flask which he said contained water but I knew from experience that it would be something stronger.

Giving our last-minute reminders about our plan to Gabriel and Ramón, we left the Bella Vista and headed east until we reached the broad thoroughfare of the Avenida Domingo Comin then headed south until we found the Calle Cotacachi on our right. It was a wide street with good footpaths on either side. There was a good moon that night so visibility was good and we walked down the street like any local inhabitant should, talking but watching every dark corner. Reaching the Avenida 10A, we turned north and counted the narrow alleyways which connected this street with its parallel neighbour with the equally businesslike name of Avenida 10B. We entered the third alley and again headed east.

We soon came upon the broader Avenida 10B, now we changed our approach. Garcia took out his long blade and I my revolver and checked that there was a round in its chamber with the safety catch off. Garcia quickly and quietly crossed over to the other side of the avenue whilst I remained in the shadows. Luckily the street was deserted at this time of night, so I could clearly see the park a short distance down the avenue; the church and mission just a few more metres along the street, its silhouette standing in contrast to the moonlit sky.

The park looked deserted. It was only a small park; triangular in shape, no more than about fifty metres long. It was entirely covered in grass and at its borders there was a small copse of medium size trees. I motioned to Garcia to cross to my side as we carefully entered the park, looking for an appropriate hiding place nearby.

Everything changed very quickly. I had a sudden impression of two figures falling from one of the trees and knocking Garcia to the ground. I heard a faint noise behind me and half-turning took a glancing blow from some blunt object to my head before I fell to the ground.

I looked up at my assailant who now stood over me. In the moonlight, I saw the grotesque face of a Jivaro[3] his blackened teeth showing in an evil grin across his dark face.

He raised his machete above his head ready to strike and I closed my eyes ready for the death blow.

There was aloud scream of pain.

But it was not mine.

I opened up my eyes and saw a long, thin shaft of steel protruding out of the Jivaro's shoulder, the blood beginning to ooze in a slow stream down

[3] A member of a tribe who live in the Amazon jungles in north eastern Peru and south eastern Ecuador. They were regarded as fearsome by Europeans and were noted for their custom of taking and shrinking heads.

his dirty poncho. The blade was withdrawn and the Jivaro dropped his machete, clutched his shoulder and fled into the darkness. The two Jivaros holding Garcia threw him to the ground and also ran off into the darkness.

I strong hand reached down and was offered to me. I turned and looked up at my rescuer who had stepped from the shadows.

"Father Xavier!" I exclaimed.

"Come, Colonel Moreno. It is all well now. Your young friend Capitán Rivera is with me and Raul and Ramón are just coming up the street. Ah! And here is the stout Garcia who has also gained his freedom!"

"Are you alright Colonel...? I mean Señor?"

I shook my head to clarify my wits before turning to my friend, "It seems that Father Xavier knows all of our names, old friend so we need not pretend any longer."

Gabriel and then Ramón suddenly appeared out of the shadows of the park. Another group of men stood at a small distance back in the shadows ready to help.

"Well, Ramón, you were certainly right about the trap! Those fellows were smarter than I thought! They got here earlier than us and we walked right into it."

"Come now, Colonel Moreno,' said Father Xavier," let us all return to the Bella Vista where I will provide you all with an excellent supper and an explanation. You seemed to have a talent, Colonel, in making the Confessor confess! Raul has his cart just down the street. Let me help you up."

Back at the Bella Vista, Ramón ushered us into his dining room and brought some bread, olives, cheese and a few bottles of his best wine from the kitchen. Outside I noticed that Raul was saying good night to the men who had been called on to assist us.

Decimocuarta Historia: Viejos Enemigos y Nuevos Amigos

Fourteenth Story: Old Enemies and New Friends.

"They were Jivaros!" I exclaimed after we had settled ourselves down in the dining room of the Bella Vista.

"Yes!" Father Xavier said, looking across the table, a glass of best claret in his hand, "cronies of your old friend Capitán Pedro Moralez. Do you remember him?"

It came as somewhat of a shock that Father Xavier knew so much about my past, including the intimate detail of the man who had captured Garcia and me all those years ago in the border jungles.

"That is a man I would never forget! His treatment of Garcia and me and our wounded men when we were captured on the border will never be erased from my memory. He commanded a group of local militia who were, in the most part Jivaros."

"The very same, but now he is Teniente Coronel Moralez – a quick series of promotions you would agree in such a short time. And his 'militia' as you give them some military credit, were a group banished from their own tribe who readily accepted the Junta's money as mercenaries. Some of them are still in the employ of that man.

There is another old acquaintance of yours also involved here. Well, you may have not personally met him as you were being…well…executed at that time," Father Xavier gave a short laugh and turned quickly to the hotel owner who was carving up another block of cheese with a big knife.

"You say, Ramón that the person who delivered the note this morning was a beautiful woman?"

"Yes Padre, a very beautiful woman with long black hair and lovely eyes and a smile which would melt any man's heart."

"Ah, that sounds like Doña Inèz López Romero – a most dangerous woman if it was her. She is indeed a cunning vixen and the mistress of our main adversary."

Turning to me, he continued: "You will recall that the Junta in Quito sent one of their most trusted men, one Capitán Carrasco Flores Martin to oversee your collective executions. He is an opportunist of the highest degree and a man who is more cunning than he is clever. It was lucky for you that he prefers the more ...umm...shall we say...the more social aspects of executions. Had it been me, I would have personally inspected the bodies, their wounds, pulses and so on and then tossed the first dirt into the graves.

Well, now, this Capitán Flores was paid off very handsomely by the Junta, promoted and retired with great honour from the military before taking up his new civilian life. He is now standing as a candidate for the post of President and has considerable support from the wealthy landowners in the country's eastern provinces. Moralez and his Jivaros are his personal assistants, shall we say, who are employed to get rid of any opposition such as yourselves."

"I am a little confused about this political situation. How could Garcia and I be involved in Flores' intrigues?" I asked.

"Well, it is a long and very old story, but if you will tolerate an old priest, then I will tell it to you. It may give you some insights into the secrets of San Rafael. Perhaps you must hear more of my story first.

The beginning of it I have already told you on our coach journey; I had resigned my commission from the army in disgust at the treatment of the indigenous people – my Grandmother's own people – and, disowned by my family had fled north to Ecuador. Here I had many menial jobs including one at the Army Headquarters in Quito tending to the horses of the officers. Remember that I was very familiar with army horses from my own training. My duties often meant some contact with the many officers stationed at headquarters and I became friends with some of them who appreciated my way around horses and my knowledge of military habits and protocol. One of them was a major who had lost an arm in 1859 in one of the country's many civil disputes. He and I often talked about the disputes then occurring with the local tribes in the Oriente[1]. There had been considerable expansion into the tribal lands to harvest rubber and naturally the indigenous people objected and attacked the workers of the Caucheros[2]. My friend the major had a great feeling for the indigenous peoples and his name was..."

[1] Ecuador's Amazonian region in the east of the country.
[2] A term meaning the 'Rubber Barons' applied to those who controlled large rubber plantations in the Amazon.

"Comandante Antonio Castillo Andrés!" I interrupted.

"The very man!" replied Xavier. "He and I became good friends and found that we both had sympathy for the poor indigenious peoples who were being exploited in many parts of the country. Unfortuately, he later fell foul of the new Junta who did not appreciate his forthright views on native exploitation so they sent him to the mountains to command the remote Supply Depot of San Rafael.

So I gave up the secular world and became a Jesuit. I was attracted to the Company because of their military style of discipline and their outreach to the poor and indigenous peoples through their missions and schools. Also, there was something about their independence which attracted me. Our Company is often accused of interferring in politics and goverment authority because we owe our alegence to his Holiness, the Pope and to our

Superior General rather than to the governments of countries. As you may remember from your history books, there was often conflict between us because of our protection of the people and the exploitating landowners who were often championed by local and national governments.

Our order was expelled from the Spanish colonies in South America in 1769 but gradually returned after the end of the Napaoleonic era in Europe in 1814. It was after that time that the ideals associated with the rights of man became a more popular political concept. Unfortunately these ideals, which were also in the minds of the liberators of our countries here in South America, were forgotten by the many newly established governments. Faced with running their own new country, the newly created governments often fell back on the old colonial realities of exploiting the people and the land for their own territorial and financial gain. Liberty, egality and freedom soon returned to the control by the rich and powerful and many of the indigenous people once more became enslaved."

Father Xavier paused for a while. His personal feelings and emotions had come to the forefront of his story, he took time to gather his thoughts before continuing.

"This is where my story returns to San Rafael, "he continued. "Here in Ecuador, my superiors soon recognised that I had many talents and contacts in high places which would be useful in our goals of helping the people. They encouraged my work and independent movement around the several countries in this part of the word. In time, and during my travels, I acquired unintentionally a strong network of friends, especially out in the country parishes. One was in Baños de Agua Santa where I was delighted to renew my friendship with Comandante Castillo. I also became good friends with his local Chaplain, Fray Dominic Vargas Mendoza. Yes, Brother Dom and

I have been old friends for many years, even though he is a Dominican." He laughed.

"I soon realised that in his wanderings in his beloved mountains as well as the military chaplain at San Rafael, Brother Dom knew more about what was going on than I could ever understand by my own travels. So, he became my agent, if you will, in that part of the country. We corresponded regularly and I kept my activities elsewhere knowing that Baños and its surrounds were in good hands.

My activities often led me into the military Headquarters in Quito where my military background in Peru was unknown. I became their Chaplain and as such was in a position to learn much about the military situation in the country. At times I would be asked by the Headquarters staff to assist in some pastoral matter further out in the countryside and my small successes led to a position of trust. My ability to move freely across borders and between social classes also meant that I could assist the Company's goals of helping the local people in any struggle that they may have with authority or landowners. Soon, my sphere of influence extended into several of our neighbouring countries, including Peru and Bolivia; places in which I had considerable experience but also where I was known by some.

During the War of the Pacific, I was still able to move freely between many of the warring factions. This is how I met our friend Roberto the bandit on our trip to Puno. Do you remember, Colonel Moreno?"

"Yes." I replied. "I thought then that there was more to the matter than just a simple priest appealing to the good nature of humankind."

"Yes, so it was. Roberto and his band had fought a guerrilla war in that part of Peru when you and Sargento Garcia were holding your ground just a little to the north."

Garcia grinned and slapped his thigh in a gesture of triumph and exclaimed loudly "I knew it!"

"Well, now!" Xavier continued, "let me cut a long story to its essentials and get back to San Rafael. As you know from your own ordeals at Baños, the powerful Junta which dominated Ecuador at the time ordered your execution and the closure of the Supply Depot at San Rafael. This was all completed to everyone's satisfaction; Comandante Castillo retired with honour, the local people gained considerable wealth and goods from the Comandante's literal following of his orders to break up the unit, and the Junta was happy that the political embarrassment of your presence had been solved.

Shortly after the Comandante's retirement to Colombia, the military Junta was thrown out by a more democratic government and since then we have had an unstable situation of short-term governments varying between liberalism and conservatism."

"And how, Padre, if I may ask, what does this have to do with our quest?" I asked, looking also at Gabriel who shrugged his shoulders suggesting that he too was in the dark.

"Ah, this is where life becomes more interesting," said Xavier with a conspiratorial grin, "our friend the Comandante always had an eye for political intrigue as I have told you. He had always been an opponent of the Junta but as a serving officer and in a remote mountain supply depot he had little influence to make any changes so he kept to himself and looked more to the local history than current events further afield.

One day I received a letter from Brother Dom telling me that the Comandante had found something at the hacienda at San Rafael which had important implications for the government. He did not know exactly what Antonio Castillo had found but that he was very excited. Unfortunately, the matter of your capture complicated the issue and the 'new development' was put aside. When that issue of your capture was successfully resolved and it looked like the government might change to a more democratic one, the Comandante put this secret matter aside and spoke of it no more.

However, a year is a long time in politics; indeed, each day sometimes means a difference and the retired soldier once was forced to recall the importance of the secret of San Rafael.

The government now was a liberal one with some politicians again asserting the need for reform and support of indigenous rights. This was well and good, but as it is often said in Ecclesiastes 10:1, there was once more 'a fly in the ointment'! This was in the person of our old friend, the overseer of executions, retired army officer and prospective politician Carrasco Flores[3] Martin

[3] This character is fictional and should not be confused with the real Ecuadorean soldier and President, Juan José Flores y Aramburu (1800 –1864).

who is now making a very strong case for being elected the next President of Ecuador.

Such a man should never have pretensions for such high office but he desires power and has the strong support from many landowners and plantation owners in the east. For their own gain, they want to push further east into the tribal lands of this country and also into Peru by extending the borders further south. Our Company here in Ecuador was unhappy when they found this out from a reliable source."

"Father Xavier, the Exploration Priest," I suggested. Xavier laughed at the modification of my own previous military title of 'Exploration Officer' in finding out the locations of the enemies of my country.

"Touché, Colonel Moreno, perhaps I did pick up a few ideas in the salons of Quito, but the matter was taken very seriously by my order. It was also by chance that Comandante Castillo had also heard such rumours through his old contacts with the military and wrote to me mentioning that there was a secret hidden in the building of his previous command which could prevent the election of this dreadful man. He also said that he was dying and needed my help in the prevention of this travesty of justice and politics. He would not say what this secret was by letter, as he suspected that his secret may be found out by others, especially Señores Flores and Moralez so he asked me to come and give him absolution.

This is where things became confused. I arrived in time to hear his confession but he died before he could tell me the entire story. He did say that he had confided in the young officer, here and had given him some important letters for you which would lead to the secret of San Rafael.

After his funeral, I returned to Quito and discussed the matter with my superiors. They fully supported the concept that Flores must be stopped and charged me with the task of giving you some unofficial support should you take up the quest to find the secret of San Rafael. It was a simple matter to take the Company's business to Cuzco where I settled down as an assistant at our order's church just across the laneway from your Universidad Nacional de San Antonio Abad del Cusco in the Plaza de Armes.

Naturally, I had some contacts at the university, including several students who were destined for our order. It did not take long to find that you had booked two coach seats to Puno so I assumed that you had taken up the quest. As you know, I also booked a seat and also had to put up with that irritating Major. I really did have some clerical business at our church in Puno, but had taken precautions in case you had decided to go beyond that city.

"The Undertaker!" I said looking at Garcia who grinned.

"I am sorry, I do not know who you mean," said Xavier with a perplexed look on his face, "I had one of my young students from Puno also take passage to his home in Bolivia at San Pablo de Tiquina should you decide to go on to La Paz. I had another contact employed at the coaching station there. The telegraph is a most useful invention."

"Ah…the shy student!" I said with satisfaction for the mystery of our coach trips had now fallen into place.

"Yes, I have strong hopes that young Diego will make an excellent member of the Company if he passes his exams," Xavier continued.

"Having had a telegram from San Pablo that you and Garcia had stopped off at Copacabana, it was only a matter of logic and the tyranny of distance which suggested that this is where you would meet up with Capitán Rivera and that your most practical course of action would be to take the sea route to Guayaquil. Of course, it was here that you met my other friends Raul and former Sargento Primero Franco. Well, then, that is the story so far."

Ramón and Raul both smiled at this mention of their part in the plot and raised their glasses to Father Xavier.

"Well, it has been a long day, señores!" stated Father Xavier getting to his feet. Considering the circumstances Colonel Moreno, might I propose that I come with you and your brave company to San Rafael? After all, I now have some capital invested in your venture and can be of further service if you should wish it?"

The looks of anticipation on the faces of my companions and my own feelings gave a quick positive response to that proposal.

"Good then!" said Xavier, "I therefore have some further work to do tonight. Ramón here will take care of our needed supplies for the journey. We will leave here tomorrow morning…say at seven? Good then, it is all settled. Buenas noches señores[4]!"

With that, Father Xavier took up his cane and walked brusquely out of the room. Tomorrow should be an interesting day.

[4] "Good night, sirs!"

Decimoquinta Historia: Bendición de los Dominicos
Fifteenth Story: The Dominican's Blessing

Sunrise at the Bella Vista was far from being beautiful; the first rays of the sun waking me from a fitful sleep after too much of the hotel's best wine. Noises below suggested that our hosts were already up and preparing for the journey.

Garcia and Gabriel were also stirring and the smell of hot bread reminded me that I was very hungry now in anticipation of our journey.

Buenos días señores[1]," came Ramón's cheerful greeting, indicating a table with bowls of hot rolls, various spreads, fruit and a steaming pot of very aromatic coffee. There were also several boxes laden with cans of food, loaves of bread, potatoes, onions and fruit. There were also two shotguns and several boxes of cartridges.

[1] Literally "Good Day" but can also mean "Good Morning" at this time of day.

Precisely at seven, a carriage pulled up outside. It was a very handsome vehicle of good size pulled by two horses. It was painted and polished a shiny black with a red trim and a very ornate coat-of-arms on its door.

Father Xavier jumped down from the seat and said with a smile: "The Bishop is a very understanding person and had no qualms about lending me his personal carriage to take some important guests out into the country."

Ramón climbed up onto the driver's seat of the coach and looked down at Father Xavier:

"Raul and I will be your drivers, Padre. My cousins Guido and Federico will be here soon to run the hotel so we will come with you. Two good men, huh?"

"Thank you, Sargento. You both will be most welcome," replied Xavier, using Ramón's former military title in appreciation of the offered help.

Father Xavier turned to me and added: "I hope that you will appreciate the extra help, Colonel Morano. Ramón and Raul were both former tough soldiers of a famous mountain regiment before they took to the dangerous occupation of running an hotel. I have used their services before and therefore know that they can be relied upon to handle a dangerous situation."

"Thank you, Padre." I replied, "with Moralez and his Jivaros at our heels, I am grateful for any help offered."

"Good! Then let us depart. It is almost two hundred kilometres up into the mountains to Baños de Agua Santa and it will probably take three days, God willing. It would be best that we travel on minor roads to avoid any questions – not to mention why the Bishop's coach should be on the road."

Father Xavier unfolded a map and placed it on the top of the wheel of the coach. We gathered round and he traced out a probable route.

"Here we are at Guayaquil. On the first day it will be easy travelling so we should make the village of Montalvo. Here. Father Juan at the Iglesia de Montalvo will be happy to put us up for the night. Next, we have a problem; there are two large towns in the way, Riobamba and Ambato and the mighty volcano Chimborazo. I think that we should avoid both these large towns in case there are spies waiting to note our passage. If we make good time, we can slip through Riobamba at nightfall and stop at the Santuario Católico de Jesús Caido at Penipe and stay with Father Carlos. From there it is but forty kilometres to Baños. What do you think, Colonel?"

Looking at the map, I could see that the chosen route would be a good one and the most direct. I looked up at Father Xavier and smiled:

"It looks like a good route Father Xavier, and it should seem appropriate that the Bishop should visit his distant flock in his beautiful carriage."

For two days we travelled in comfort. The Bishop's carriage had been especially well-sprung so that his Excellency would not feel the many holes in the rough country roads. In both the small towns at which we spent our nights, the Reverend Fathers were happy to see Father Xavier as they knew him to be a good man and one with some authority back in Quito; he was well-known in many country parishes for helping the local clergy with their many schools and missions. At both towns, the good Fathers soon found accommodation for us all and insisted in adding to our plentiful stocks of food and wine. Garcia was most grateful to Father Carlos at Penipe for a large jar of his locally-brewed and famous chicha.

On the third day, we crossed the old stone bridge over the Rio Bascún not far from where it joined the larger Rio Pastaza. Here it was a narrow stream in a wider boulder-strewn valley which could be treacherous in times of flood. The Pastaza became wider and faster flowing as it found its way down the mountains and into the mighty Rio Marañón some five hundred kilometres away in the Amazon Basin.

The sun had long drifted over the mountains behind us as we slowly entered Baños de Agua Santa, the vast slopes of the volcano Mama Tungurahua[2] hidden from us by the nearby hills and the clouds above.

Perhaps some of the locals going about their business in the twilight may have wondered why such a magnificent carriage with the mark of the Bishop of Guayaquil on its doors should enter their town, but then again, perhaps not. Baños de

[2] El volcán Tungurahua is an active volcano with the city of Baños de Agua Santa on its northern slopes. The name 'Tungurahua' comes from the Quechua for 'Throat of Fire' but the locals often refer to the mountain as 'Mama Tungurahua' with some reverence.

Agua Santa was after all, a place of religious significance and an end point for pilgrims from all over the country. When we pulled up outside the small stone church in the central plaza, their questions would have been answered and they would have pulled their sombreros down over their eyes and continued on their way.

"Come!" said Father Xavier opening the door of the coach, "you have another old friend to meet in the Rectory. Ramón and Raul will take care of the bags."

With that he stepped down and walked through the small gate and down the path which led to the large rectory which had been built next to the church. It was an old, stone house with a single wide veranda fronting the street which opened out to the well-ordered gardens of the plaza beyond.

Sitting in a chair with a blanket wrapped around his legs was Fray Dominic[3]. The old man saw Father Xavier and tried to rise using a walking stick which he had by his chair but the Jesuit motioned him to remain seated. He was overjoyed to see his old friend after so many years. As Garcia and I came up the stairs he looked with some astonishment; tears of happiness began to roll down his wrinkled brown face.

"Don Hernán and Sargento Pablo!" he cried, reaching out his arms, "is it really you? And look! The young Teniente Rivera also!"

"Yes, old friend, both of us back from the dead! And with our young gaoler returning the bodies back to you," I replied with joy.

Brother Dom settled back in his chair and pulled the blanked higher up onto his legs. "Please

[3] 'Fray' is a Spanish title used by Friars and can be used to mean 'Brother'

forgive me! I would like to jump up and embrace all of you but my legs are determined to stay in this accursed chair."

"It is alright, my old friend," I said quietly and Garcia came up and gave the old Brother a strong embrace.

Xavier had found several small chairs and placed them in front of Brother Dominic who looked at me and then at Garcia and gave a hearty laugh.

"Ha! I gave you the Last Rites…well that was what they should have been if you were really dying, but as the execution was a sham, I thought that they might have been inappropriate."

"Yes!" I replied with a smile. "As I recall, you made a very exaggerated Sign of the Cross and whispered something like 'Usque mane. Vos esse supponitur, mortuus est![4]"

[4] Latin: 'Stay down. You are supposed to be dead!'

Father Xavier laughed out loud thinking that such a substitute for the Last Rites was very funny and commented: "Ah! Some good Latin, Fray Dominic. I must use it when I am not sure of the bona fides of my next recipient."

"Well it was intended for that buffoon from Quito, who probably wouldn't know his Horace from his horse!"

Laughter from all of us, including Garcia who knew no Latin but caught the meaning of the old Brother's jibe.

Brother Dominic picked up a small bell which was on his side table and rang it. A rather young seminarian part fell and part walked out from a nearby door where he was obviously curious about the new visitors who came to this small town in a Bishop's carriage.

"Ah, here is my young acolyte who can now help with the service. Desiderio, would you bring my guests some of my provisions from my personal store?" Dominic said with a wink of his eye to Father Xavier.

Desiderio grinned and quickly turned and left the veranda. He soon returned with several bottles of good wine, glasses and a plate full of cheese and other delicious items which he placed on the small side table.

"Dominic looked up and spread his hands in depreciation. "Now that I am retired, I am well looked after by the good Sisters but sometimes an old man needs something extra other than the simple rectory fare. So, I have my own supply, you understand. Please drink, eat."

Xavier filled the old man's glass and then in turn our glasses and lastly his own. "Yes Dom, that is true but if I know Mother Superior Gerarda well, she would have found out your secret long ago but prefers to maintain it rather than listen to your complaints."

"You may be correct Father Xavier," he replied "and I do rather like some peace and quiet …on rare occasions, but tell me for I am curious, why have you brought back two dead men and their executioner back to our little town of Baños?"

"It is a long story, Dom," Xavier replied," but it concerns San Rafael and the story that Don Antonio used to talk about all those years ago when we all had partaken of too much wine."

"Ah yes, his little 'secret of San Rafael'! He never did get to the final story of exactly what that secret happened to be. It was probably for the best when he closed down the supply depot and went into retirement but it may have made a good story."

"It did indeed, but as yet we only know some of it and the Comandante only left a few cryptic clues." Xavier then gave the old Brother a brief explanation of how we had all come to meet and of our separate journeys. I also told him about the possibility that Colonel Moralez and his Jivaros may also come to San Rafael to find the Comandante's secret.

At that moment, Ramón and Raul came up the steps and sat down on the low parapet of the veranda. "We have put the horses in the church's barn if that is alright with you, Brother," Ramón said to Dominic.

"That is good, señor. I am sure that the good Sisters would approve, especially with the Bishop's carriage parked outside. I am Fray Dominic by the way, but my friends simply call me Dom."

I introduced our two good friends who had done a sterling job driving the coach and caring for us in Guayaquil. Both men beamed at the praise which they had been given.

Ramón thanked me and turned to Brother Dominic: "If it is permitted...Dom.... may Raul and I sleep in the barn? It is too beautiful a carriage to be left alone and we must also tend to the horses in the morning if we need to start early."

"Good idea! but for now, come! have some wine and we will talk of old times," said Dom passing over two more glasses and one of the bottles of wine. "My secret supply is well-stocked, thanks to the generosity of Comandante Antonio and the wine cellar of San Rafael."

When told of the Comandante's passing, Dominic was downcast for a while and then looked up with a benign smile and raised his glass. "Señores! Here is a toast to a great man. May he rest in peace!"

We all raised our glasses and Xavier made the Sign of the Cross to honour his late friend.

"Come now!" said Brother Dom, "the night is still young and we are all friends here. Baños is a small town and everyone knows everyone else…and all of them are God's children whom I have been caring for all of these years. We are safe here, tonight. Tomorrow you shall all have a good breakfast because I am sure that you will want to go out to the old hacienda as soon as Inti comes over the mountain."

"Yes, Dom, that is the idea if you don't mind our leaving you so quickly, for it is imperative that we get to San Rafael before others decide to intervene," Xavier said.

"Do not worry about them!" Dominic said with an enigmatic smile, "I have many friends here in town and out in the country. In the morning I will send Desiderio out to talk to his friends. Many of them are what you might call delincuentes[5] but they are good boys really…a bit high spirited perhaps, but they have helped me on many occasions. Desiderio was one of them but now he

---

[5] delinquents

is on the right path. His friends will watch the road into town as well as the coaching station and the inns. They will tell us if any strangers come into town. Come now! fill your glasses and forget tomorrow."

"Let us hope that Moralez and his men are slow in coming." Xavier said.

Dominic looked at him over the rim of his glass and said with a mischievous smile: "Ah! You Jesuits! You are like grocers…you weigh everything! If your order had their way, we would all be on your payroll. Who knows! Perhaps one day we might even have a Jesuit Pope!"

"And he will be a South American![6]" added Garcia who was now into his fourth glass of wine.

---

[6] The current Pope, Pope Francis is both a Jesuit and from Argentina.

"The world could do well with that arrangement!" Xavier replied, "but you Dominicans would have to be on your toes!" he laughed.

Garcia leaned across the table and gave a conspiratorial wink at Dominic. "I was told once about a time during the wars of Independence that a Dominican, a Franciscan and a Jesuit fighting against the Spanish, were captured and locked up in a goal." It was good to see Garcia relax now that he was in the company of his friend Dominic as both men had hard lives and enjoyed each other's company. He continued with his story:

"Like the Blessed Saint Peter, they were locked away and their lives threatened. The poor Franciscan fell to his knees and prayed a simple prayer that they might be delivered. The Dominican found some charcoal on the floor and composed a rich sermon on the bare wall based on the Captivity of the Saint. But the Jesuit!

…well, he borrowed the Franciscan's rosary and used it to pick the cell's lock and freed them all!"

There was laughter all around at this joke and Xavier wiped the tears from his eyes and replied: "A good Jesuit today in these uncertain times would be probably carrying his own set of lock picks!"

More laughter.

The food, the wine and the lateness of the evening was beginning to take their toll on the travellers and the old friar. Dominic looked around at his friends and rang his small bell.

"I will have Desiderio show you to your cells, if I can add a pun to Garcia's little story, but be assured that there will be no bars! In the morning you shall all have your good breakfast and go out to find the secret of San Rafael. Now I will give you all a blessing and we can go to our beds."

Dominic held up his hand and closed his eyes and said quietly: "Deus, dona nobis bonam noctis somnus una oculi aperti ad inimicos nostros[7]."

An "Amen" came from Father Xavier and we stood up and thanked the old Dominican for his generosity. Desiderio was waiting at the main door to take us to our rooms for a well-earned rest.

[7] Latin: "God, grant us a good night's sleep with one eye open for our enemies."

Dieciséis Historia: El Secreto de San Rafael
Sixteenth Story: The Secret of San Rafael

Very early the next morning, we said our farewells to Brother Dom and climbed into the carriage which Ramón and Raul had brought around to the front of the rectory. They had spent some time in removing the dust from the previous day's travel and were now sitting up on the drivers' seat. I noticed that Raul cradled his shotgun in his arms and Ramón held the reins but his weapon was ready at hand down the side of the seat.

"Buenos días, señores!" Ramón hailed from above. There were several good-natured replies but Garcia and Gabriel did not seem to have yet greeted the morning.

"Never mind, my friends!" I said slapping Garcia on the back, "Ch'aska Quyllur[1] is here to greet

[1] Quechua for the Incan goddess of the dawn and of the twilight – associated with the planet Venus.

you and a good coach ride into the country will soon clear the cobwebs of the night!"

With us all on board, and a few directions from Xavier, Ramón headed the carriage down the cobbles of the Calle Oriente, which as its name suggests ran eastwards out of the town, and onto the main road. This followed the Rio Pastaza down its steep-sided valley which eventually opened out into the Amazon Basin. A short distance along the main road, we turned off at a dusty side road which was signed by a large rock 'El Camino Real' – the royal road. There was no longer any royal significance to this narrow, dusty road other than it had once been the route which the Inca and his retinue would have taken from the sacred warm springs of Baños down to his jungle province of Antisuyu[2]. It also was the road to the old hacienda of San Rafael.

[2] The Incan Empire, which they called in Quechua, *'Tawantinsuyu'* or "The Four Regions" consisted of the *'suyu'* (regions) of *Chinchaysuyu* (north), *Antisuyu* (east; the Amazon jungle), *Qullasuyu* (south) and *Kuntisuyu* (west).

Xavier leaned across the carriage so that he could be heard by Gabriel and me: "The hacienda of San Rafael was built in the late eighteenth century by a Spanish nobleman Don Gervasio de León, who saw that this region would control much of the trade going from the wealth of the Amazon Basin to Quito. He was only moderately successful in taking a share in this trade but the hacienda stayed in his family until it was taken over after the death of the last of the line. Following independence in 1820, there had been several owners but the estate generally fell into disrepair until the army decided to take it over in the early 1880's as a supply depot in support of their push into the Amazon Basin. The last owner was one Colonel Juan Serrano Tupahuaca, another mestizo who was a former aid-de-camp to General José María Urvina[3]. The Colonel was given this estate by the general who had been born not far from here, near Ambato. When Urvina became

[3] **José María Mariano Segundo de Urvina y Viteri** (1808 – 1891) was a sailor and soldier and President of Ecuador from 13 July 1851 to 16 October 1856. Sometimes his surname is spelt 'Urbina'.

President in 1851, he freed all of the slaves and tried to bring in many reforms. Colonel Serrano, because of his Incan ancestry, had a very good and close relationship with the local people, the Puruhuaes and the Chachapoyas or cloud warriors, of northern Peru. That is all I know about the hacienda of San Rafael and whatever the Comandante found there is still a mystery to me."

It did not take too long before we reached the hacienda. I remember the first time Garcia and I arrived there; as prisoners tied up in the back of a supply wagon. The gates had been opened and we had been greeted by the Comandante who was appalled at our rough treatment and ordered his staff to treat us like honoured guests. Now one of the gates hung down from its broken hinges and the other was fully opened. Raul drove the carriage carefully through the gate and into the courtyard. It showed none of the military order of that past time. Some of masonry of the walls had been broken and now weeds grew along the edges of the buildings. Most of the doors which had not been removed were wide open. We expected that the interior had also suffered accordingly, as the Comandante had taken his order to disband the Supply Depot of San Rafael to mean dismantle it. Consequently, anything of value, including some of the timbers and stone of the building itself had been taken away by its former soldiers and the local civilians. There would not be many peasant farmer's homes around Baños which would not contain some relic of the old hacienda. All of its content, minus some military supplies which were sent back to Ambato to show that the order of disbandment had been carried out, had been removed. All of the furniture which had been minimal anyway, the food, most of the blankets and tableware and of course, the contents of Don Antonio's good wine cellar had been removed years ago.

Ramón and Raul unloaded our supplies in what had been the old kitchen. At least the old stone oven remained and there would be enough scrap timber around to have a warm fire. This would be our headquarters as it commanded a good view of the gate and was small enough to defend if needs be. Ramón approached Xavier with his shotgun couched loosely in his arms:

"Padre, with your permission and that of Don Hernán, it may be advisable that Raul and I leave the carriage here in the stable and then go down the road and find a nice protected shelter where we can watch the approaches from the east. Our enemies may do as we did and avoid the main roads and come up from the jungle."

Ramón was now the experienced soldier who saw all of the approaches to his position as potential threats. The road from the east coming from the direction of the Amazon Basin was the same one along which Garcia and I had been brought to the hacienda and the same one down which we had secretly left. We had left Moralez and his Jivaros back in Guayaquil and it would be most likely that they would follow us along the roads from that city. However, the east was Jivaro territory and whilst the road to Baños was the only one through the mountains this far north, it made good sense to keep a watch in that direction.

Ramón and Raul made up a small pack of supplies and with their shotguns under their arms waved us farewell as they walked out of the hacienda to take up a hidden camp further down the road.

The four of us moved into the old kitchen and attempted to make our new home both comfortable and secure. Luckily the old well which was in a small courtyard off the kitchen was still in good working order.

Being back at San Rafael, regardless of its now distressed appearance gave me a feeling of emptiness and a mind full of eerie sensations. San Rafael had once been our prison but it also had been filled with the laughter and joy of several families; wives and children of the local soldiers who were employed at the depot. Now there was nothing but silence and hostility save for the small comfort of our kitchen.

We ate a very brief lunch and decided that there was no time to waste in looking for the secret of the hacienda. We went upstairs to the Comandante's old dining room. For it was here, as stated in his cryptic letter that we had often spent the evening over cigars and his fine Amontillado. Our search would begin here.

Each of us took one of the four walls and searched for some small alcove or other clue which might lead the way. Even the old bookcases built into the wall had no secret lever or door to open. The wood panels were sounded but all appeared to be solid. The flagstones of the floor contain no secret cypher nor ring which could be opened to reveal a secret stairway. Garcia went into the old, ornate fireplace and climbed part of the way up to search for a hidden shelf. He emerged like some blackened chimney urchin with only the whites of his eyes showing through the black grime.

I opened the letter and re-read its contents. There was only the passage left to give us some clues:

"Forasmuch as ye are manifestly declared to be the epistle of Christ ministered by us, written not with ink, but with the Spirit of the living God; not in tables of stone, but in fleshy tables of the heart."

What did it mean? There was nothing in the room which could have been interpreted as an object of this passage. There were no 'tables of stone'; the original long oak table had long ago been broken up for firewood in some farmer's cottage.

Xavier took the letter and studied it closely. He had only had a brief inspection of it following our meeting at Guayaquil. He read it to himself quietly; his lips moving with some deliberation through the text.

"Of course, this is a Bible passage, but it makes no sense in the context of this barren room. Let me think. Yes!" he exclaimed with some excitement. "It comes from Corinthians."

He read the passage through again and then held his head up as though looking for something in his mind."

"2 Corinthians, I think." He closed his eyes and muttered some words quietly from that Book of the Bible. "I have it! 2 Corinthians, Chapter Three and Verse Three: Fac ut locutus es: manifestati quod epistola estis Christi ministrata a nobis, scripta non atramento, sed Spiritu Dei vivi: non in tabulis lapideis, sed in tabulis carneis cordis" he recited the passage again in his familiar Latin. "Now what would that mean?"

I looked around the room hoping that the identification of the passage would offer some clue. My eye came to rest on something from my classical studies: "The fireplace!" I exclaimed.

"The supporting columns of the mantelpiece are Corinthian Columns. Look there!"

The others turned around to where I was pointing. Xavier ran up to the fireplace and said: "2 Corinthians…perhaps the second column? Look, it is divided up into three sections!"

He took hold of the third stone up from the base and pushed with all of his might. Nothing. He pushed again, this time from the side and he noticed a small movement.

"Look!" he said with some excitement "it does not push in but rotates! The column is divided into separate vertical segments, three rotations of this stone perhaps!"

Grasping the round section of the column, he rotated it through one turn of a segment, then the other and finally the third. Within the column there was an audible 'click' and Xavier was able to pull the loose section of the column outwards.

"What a clever arrangement!" he exclaimed and got down on his knees to look into the hole formed by the missing piece of the column. Reaching in, he extracted a long, brass cylinder covered with cobwebs. There was a screw cap on one end which opened after several turns. There was an old parchment inside.

"Come, my friends! Let us go down to the kitchen where we can spread it out on the stone workbench," he cried.

Shadows were beginning to creep across the courtyard as we hurriedly descended the outside stairs and ran across to the kitchen. Xavier carefully pulled the parchment out of its holder and spread it out on the top of the old marble work bench. Garcia had found several stones to hold down the edges of the document.

It was thankfully in modern Spanish and looked like some important legal document. There was a large, official red seal at the bottom on the yellowed paper bearing the coat of arms of Ecuador. The main signature below it was that of José María Mariano Segundo de Urvina y Viteri, the former President. The signature below it was that of the witness to the document, Don Gervasio de León y Castille, the former owner of the hacienda.

Gabriel looked closer at the document as only a trained lawyer would. He looked up suddenly and exclaimed: "Why, this is the famous Treaty of Ambato or at least a hand-written copy of it!"

We looked at him with little understanding and so he continued: "Don't you see? This is the document which President Urvina signed to free the slaves and Indians back in 1851! Look, here are the marks of the tribes in the neighbouring part of the Amazon Basin who agreed to this treaty."

"Of course!" Xavier exclaimed with considerable excitement. "This is why Flores Martin and his bootlicker Moralez are so interested in San Rafael and your search for its secret. For most of the year, Flores has been waging a campaign against our more liberal government. He, with the support of a strong group of wealthy landowners has been advocating further economic expansion into the Amazon Basin; both in this country and in northern Peru."

I sat down on the side of the bench and looked at the document. "But surely this document would prevent this from happening. It would be enshrined in the current government's records, surely?"

"No! That is just the problem," exclaimed Xavier "the previous Junta destroyed many of the state's documents which were against their interests. The current government has a recollection of this document of course, but without the actual document, Flores could mount a very strong legal argument that this treaty no longer exists"

"That is so!" Gabriel the lawyer interjected, "Señor Flores could openly challenge the existence of the treaty and win popular support for his proposed opening up of Amazonia for the good of the country. With the backing of his wealthy supporters who would benefit from such expansion, he could become President and the indigenous peoples of both Ecuador and northern Peru would be displaced."

"This is indeed a most important discovery!" I said, "and one which our friend Moralez would want to get hold of for his patron."

"I'm so glad that you agree, Colonel Moreno." The cold, clear voice came from the open door of the kitchen. Standing there was the gaunt figure of Pedro Moralez; a Colt revolver in his hand.

"Move away from the table and put your hands where I can see them, señores. Ah, that's better! Now I can come into your humble abode. You will of course remember my assistant, Santiago,

Father Xavier. His shoulder has not yet healed but he is just as effective in using his machete with his left hand. You will of course, place your cane on the table."

The big Jivaro grinned and waved his weapon above his head with a glint of triumph in his eyes.

"I must say, Colonel that you make a very fine-looking corpse and not what I had expected after Don Carrasco had described your execution here those many years ago. No matter. I will soon correct that error.

We had all retreated to the other side of the marble work bench on which sat the important document. Garcia had raised his arms so that his hands were behind his head in an act of submission. He had an expression of the 'terrified native' on his broad face; a false expression which I had seen him use when we were in trouble and held by enemies. I knew what he was going to do next as he had two throwing knives in a pouch just behind his neck under his raised collar. There was very little movement obvious to our assailants as Garcia slowly wrapped the fingers of his right hand around the upward-pointing blade of one of his knives.

My hands were at my side and I wondered how fast I could be to brush my coat aside and draw my Smith & Wesson pistol before Moralez fired his weapon. Xavier had placed his cane-sword onto the table and was wondering very much the same about his weapon. Gabriel was unarmed but stood like a coiled spring ready to jump.

It all happened in a split second. There was the sudden 'boom' of a shotgun blast just outside the door and Moralez and Santiago turned suddenly at the sound. It was the distraction that Garcia wanted and he threw his knife which impaled the right forearm of Moralez who dropped his pistol with a loud cry of pain. I quickly drew my pistol as Santiago raised his machete to a throwing position. I shot him between his vicious eyes and he fell to the floor, dead. Moralez was too quick for my second shot and he dashed out of the kitchen door and into the darkness. There was another loud 'boom' of a shotgun and Ramón burst into the kitchen his gun level and another cartridge already being loaded. He relaxed when he saw the big Jivaro's body on the ground and the four of us standing behind the table.

"I am sorry, Padre. I got one of them who was waiting outside but the man who come out of the kitchen took me by surprise and I only had time to take quick aim and get off my shot. It was dark and I think that I missed him."

Raul entered, wiping his long knife on a dirty handkerchief and said with an evil grin, "Well we do not have to worry about the Jivaro left at the gate as sentry and I see that there is another here as well," he said seeing the body of Santiago on the floor. "Ramón and I dispatched another one outside of the hacienda after we followed this little party from down the valley."

"Yes!' said Ramón. "We saw them coming up the road from the east. They must have taken the southern road and come up through Puyo. They would have been waiting somewhere down the valley for some time until they could come at nightfall. I thought that the one European and four Jivaros probably meant you some harm so we followed them at a respectful distance."

"It's good that you did, Ramón," said Father Xavier. "It could have been very unfortunate for us had all of them decided to come at once. It's a pity that you missed Colonel Moralez. He may yet prove difficult."

Gabriel shook himself and came around from the other side of the table and looked at the body of the dead Jivaro. He had never seen a dead man before despite his years in the army. He looked up with a solemn expression and said: "I think that the Colonel will have some difficulty for himself in the future. When we take this document back to Quito and I hand it to the appropriate people in the government, I feel that Señor Flores' days as a politician will be numbered. There are several people in very high places who will be thankful to you for thwarting his attempts at securing the Presidency and I am sure that he and Moralez would need to find other climates well away from Ecuador."

"Well and good!" said Xavier turning to Ramón, "let us bury the Jivaros …perhaps I might even extend the Last Rites to them for all the good, it will do them in the next life. Then we can all head back to Baños. Are you up to a night drive, Raul?"

"After tonight Padre, I would drive this carriage to Hell and back!"

"I think that we have had enough of that, already, Raul. Baños will do for the time being."

"So, this is the end of our quest!" I said. "The Comandante was wise to ask us to intervene on his behalf and find the secret of San Rafael."

"Amen!" said Father Xavier as he made the Sign of the Cross.

About the Author

Hernán Eduardo Moreno Ruiz is, like this story, fictional. Had he really lived, one would find that he was born in Cuzco, Peru about 1844, the only son of Don Bernardo Moreno Fuentes, a minor politician and Doña Valentina Sisa Yupanqui who could trace her ancestry back to the Incan nobility. His father died when Hernán was about five years old and he was raised by his mother with the help of her family in reduced circumstances. He was admitted to the Universidad Nacional de San Antonio Abad del Cuzco and went on to achieve his Doctorate and a position as lecturer in the Philosophy Faculty. In addition, he volunteered for the part-time Militia and was commissioned into a local infantry regiment, becoming an Exploring Officer – an independent intelligence gatherer. After returning from the adventures at San Rafael, Moreno and Garcia again retired from active duty; Moreno to his teaching of Philosophy at the university and Garcia to his nearby farm. Both remained good friends and spent the rest of their lives devoted to their families.

About the Compiler of this Book

Although given as the compiler of these letters, Dr. Peter Terrence Scott is the actual author using the non de plume of Hernán Moreno Ruiz. He has many similarities to his fictional hero; raised and educated in Sydney, Australia, then graduating as a Science Teacher to begin a successful career of over forty years in high schools and universities. Studying at various universities part time, he achieved a Bachelor of Science, Masters Degrees in Science (Geology) and Educational Administration and a Doctorate in Education. He, too, volunteered for the Army Reserve in support of his friends who had been conscripted during the Vietnam War and was commissioned into the infantry.

After retiring from teaching he has visited all seven continents including South America several times. Here he and his wife travelled extensively visiting, his daughter-in-law's family in the high Andes and also many of the places mentioned in this book.

He now lives in Brisbane, Australia with his wife and their sons and families and their grandchildren. He is the author of over twenty books on Earth Science, Environmental Science and several works of fiction.

Dr Scott at Baños de Agua Santa, 2011

Other Books by the Author

FICTION

Letters from San Rafael (as Hernan Moreno Ruiz). Set in South America in the 1880's, this is a collection of letters smuggled home by Don Hernan Moreno, an Intelligence officer of the Peruvian Army who has been captured by the Ecuadorans during a border dispute. Taken to the fortified hacienda in Banos, in the mountains of Ecudor, he and his sargeant, Garcia, are treated as honoured guests. Each of the ten stories tells of the life and times of people in the hacienda and beyond. The final chapter is the climax of the entire book.

The Ice Ship. Set mainly in the Antarctic in the 1840's, this is the story of the survival of the crew of the futuristic auxiliary steam whaler, the AUSTRALIS which has become trapped in the ice following its voyage south along the Antarctic Peninsula. Based upon actual observations and experience of the author during a 2011 voyage into the same region on a small ex-research vessel.

The Innocence of Tom Shipley is the first novel about young teacher Tom Shipley. It begins during his days at High School and his penchant as a Laboratory Prefect in making explosives and other prankish devices, follows him through similar acts at Teachers College and then out into his first appointment at age nineteen into the profession of teaching. At a brand-new school in Canberra, he finds that as the sole Science teacher, he is now the Acting Head of Department charged with establishing this subject at the school and equipping and managing several laboratories and new incoming staff.

Tom Shipley's War is a sequel to the INNOCENCE of TOM SHIPLEY and is about the young man's protest against those who protested about National Servicemen who were called up for the Vietnam War. He volunteers for the local Citizens' Military Forces unit (later the Army Reserve) and finds another war entirely: one with the more conservative members of the Army who still believe in WW2 tactics. Based on the author's own experiences as a young officer.

NON-FICTION

Adventures in Earth Science is an in-depth, traditional Earth Science textbook on Geology, Meteorology, Oceanography and Astronomy. The latest scientific information has been given in the text including chapters on climate change and the future use of fuels and energy. The book contains over 700 pages, 1200 photographs and illustrations mostly taken by the author. It also includes 32 video links taken by the author to explain various skills as well as excursions to many exotic places in support of the text. Also has companion **Teachers' Guide** and **Laboratory Manual**.

The contents of this book have also been rearranged into the **Adventures in Earth Science Series** of eight smaller individual books in both electronic and A5 print editions.

Exploration Science	Fossils- Life in the Rocks	Riches from the Earth	A Dangerous Planet: Volcanoes & Earthquakes

| Rocks - Building The Earth | Changing the Surface: Weathering & Erosion | Through Sea & Sky: Oceanography & Meteorology | Beyond Planet Earth: Astronomy |

Adventures in Earth and Environmental Science is a two-volume textbook on the environment, how it is monitored and implications for the future. They come in electronic format and as A4-sized print editions with a **Laboratory Manual** for each volume and a **Teachers' Guide**.

Surviving Global Warming - A Guide for the Future is a comprehensive explanation of the natural and man-made causes of global warming with data from a wide range of reputable scientific bodies such as CSIRO and NASA. Written with many innovative suggestions for coping with the consequences of future global warming at the home, local and government levels. It comes as an electronic or printed edition.

A Pocketbook for Hiking and Survival is a concise reference book on going into the wild places of the Earth based on the author's extensive experience as a hiker, caver, geologist, Infantry Officer, ski instructor and leader of several youth groups. Topics include basic equipment, food, water, shelter, rope work, navigation and communications. The book is designed to be carried in pocket or backpack to where mobile phone signals may be lost. It is available in Kindle format as well as paperback and it is recommended that mobile phone users install it as a stand-alone document.

All of these books are available in electronic format for any PC or tablet in Kindle format which can be read on any device using the free Kindle App. Or as print editions. Available at all Internet book outlets or from **Felix Publishing** by contacting them at:

info.felixpublishing@gmail.com